"My head is telling me it's a completely ridiculous idea to kiss you again."

Caidy gazed at him for a long, silent moment, her eyes huge and her lips slightly parted. "And does your heart have other ideas? I hope so."

"The kids—" Ben said, rather ridiculously.

"—are busy watching a show and paying absolutely no mind to us in here," she finished.

He took a step forward, almost against his will. "This thing between us is crazy."

"Completely insane," she agreed.

"I don't know what's wrong with me."

"Probably the same thing that's wrong with me," she murmured, her voice husky and low. She took a step forward, as well, until she was only a breath away, until he was intoxicated by the scent of her, fresh and clean and lovely.

He had to kiss her. It seemed as inevitable as the sunrise over the mountains.

Dear Reader,

I have to admit, I love Christmas music. I have a huge collection and sometimes start listening to my favorites as early as October (and sometimes in March and April when I'm writing a December book!). The familiar melodies instantly set a mood of quiet peace in my home.

Caidy Bowman loves Christmas music also, though the songs in her heart have been silent since a tragedy in her past. Since the moment I came up with the idea for the Bowman siblings, Caidy has been the character whose story I've been most excited to write. Caidy lost both parents when she was young. Worse, she has blamed herself all these years for setting off the events that led to their deaths. Since then, she has given up her own dreams in order to help her family—until a new veterinarian moves into the Cold Creek area with his children. I loved writing Caidy's and Ben's story! They are two people who very much deserve to find a little comfort and joy and I was thrilled to give them a happy ending.

Wishing for a joyous holiday season for you and a wonderful new year!

All my best,

RaeAnne

A COLD CREEK NOEL

RAEANNE THAYNE

HARLEQUIN®

entertain, enrich, inspire™

Recycling programs
for this product may
not exist in your area.

ISBN-13: 978-0-373-65710-0

A COLD CREEK NOEL

www.Harlequin.com

Printed in U.S.A.

Books by RaeAnne Thayne

RAEANNE THAYNE

finds inspiration in the beautiful northern Utah mountains, where she lives with her husband and three children. Her books have won numerous honors, including RITA® Award nominations from Romance Writers of America and a Career Achievement Award from *RT Book Reviews*. RaeAnne loves to hear from readers and can be contacted through her website, www.raeannethayne.com.

To Tennis and Kjersten Watkins, with love.
We can't wait to see what life has in store for the two of you!

Chapter One

"Come on, Luke. Come on, buddy. Hang in there."

Her wipers beat back the sleet and snow as Caidy Bowman drove through the streets of Pine Gulch, Idaho, on a stormy December afternoon. Only a few inches had fallen but the roads were still dangerous, slick as spit. For only a moment, she risked lifting one hand off the steering wheel of her truck and patting the furry shape whimpering on the seat beside her.

"We're almost there. We'll get you fixed up, I swear it. Just hang on, bud. A few more minutes. That's all."

The young border collie looked at her with a trust she didn't deserve in his black eyes and she frowned, her guilt as bitter and salty as the solution the snowplows had put down on the roads.

Luke's injuries were *her* fault. She should have been watching him. She knew the half-grown pup had a curious streak a mile wide—and a tendency not to listen to her when he had an itch to investigate something.

She was working on that obedience issue and they had made good strides the past few weeks, but one moment of inattention could be disastrous, as the past hour had amply demonstrated. She didn't know if it was arrogance on her part, thinking her training of him was enough, or just irresponsibility. Either way, she should have kept him far away from Festus's pen. The bull was ornery as a rattlesnake on a hot skillet and didn't take kindly to curious young border collies nosing around his turf.

Alerted by Luke's barking and then the bull's angry snort, she had raced to old Festus's pen just in time to watch Luke jig the wrong way and the bull stomp down hard on his haunches with a sickening crunch of bone.

Her hands tightened on the steering wheel and she cursed under her breath as the last light before the vet's office turned yellow when she was still too far away to gun through it. She was almost tempted to keep going. Even if she were nabbed for running a red light by Pine Gulch's finest, she could probably talk her way out of a ticket, considering her brother was the police chief and would certainly understand this was an emergency. If she were pulled over, though, it would mean an inevitable delay and she just didn't have time for that.

The light finally changed and she took off fast, the back tires fishtailing on the icy road. She would just have to trust the salt bags she carried for traction in the bed of the pickup would do the job. Even the four-wheel drive of the truck was useless against black ice.

Finally, she reached the small square building that held the Pine Gulch Veterinary Clinic and pulled the pickup to the side doors where she knew it was only a short transfer inside to the treatment area.

She briefly considered carrying him in by herself, but it had taken the careful efforts of both her and her brother Ridge to slide a blanket under Luke and lift him into the seat of her pickup. They could bring out the stretcher and cart, she decided.

She rubbed Luke's white neck. "I'm going to go get some help, okay? You just hold tight."

He made a small whimper of pain and she bit down hard on her lip as her insides clenched with fear. She loved the little guy, even if he was nosy as a crow and even smarter, which was probably why his stubbornness was such a frustration.

He trusted her to take care of him and she refused to let him die.

She hurried to the front door, barely noticing the wind-driven sleet that gouged at her even under her Stetson.

Warm air washed over her when she opened the door, familiar with the scent of animals and antiseptic mixed in a stomach-churning sort of way with new paint.

"Hey, Caidy." A woman in green scrubs rushed to the door. "You made good time from the River Bow."

"Hi, Joni. I may have broken a few traffic laws, but this is an emergency."

"After you called, I warned Ben you were on your way and what the situation was. He's been getting ready for you. I'll let him know you've arrived."

Caidy waited, feeling the weight of each second ticking away. The new vet had only been in town a few weeks and already he had made changes to the clinic. Maybe she was just being contrary, but she had liked things better when Doc Harris ran the place. The whole

reception area looked different. The cheerful yellow
walls had been painted over with a boring white and
the weathered, comfortable, old eighties-era couch and
chairs were gone, replaced by modern benches covered in a slate vinyl that probably deflected anything
a veterinarian's patients could leak on it. A display of
Christmas gifts appropriate for pets, including a massive stocking filled to the top with toys and a giant
rawhide bone that looked as if it came from a dinosaur,
hung in one corner.

Most significant, the reception area used to sit out in
the open but it was now stuck behind a solid half wall
topped with a glass partition.

It made sense to modernize from an efficiency point
of view, but she had found the comfortably worn look
of the office before more appealing.

Not that she cared about any of that right now, with
Luke lying out in her truck, cold and hurt and probably afraid.

She shifted impatiently. Where was the man? Trim-
ming his blasted nails? Only a few moments had passed
but every second delay was too much. Just when she
was about call out to Joni to see what was taking so
long, the door into the treatment area opened and the
new vet appeared.

"Where's the dog?" he asked abruptly, and she had
only a vague impression of a frowning dark-haired man
in blue scrubs.

"Still out in my truck."

He narrowed his gaze. "Why? I can't treat him out
there."

She wanted to take that giant rawhide bone out of
that stocking and bean him with it. "Yes, I'm aware of
that," she said, fighting down her frustration. "I didn't

want to move him. I'm afraid something might be broken."

"I thought he was gored."

She wasn't sure what, exactly, she had said in that frantic call to let Joni know she was on her way.

"He did end up on the business end of a bull at some point. I'm not sure if that was before or after that bull stepped on him."

His mouth tightened. "A young dog has no business running wild in the same vicinity as a dangerous bull."

His criticism stung far too close to her own guilt for comfort. "We're a working ranch at the River Bow, Dr. Caldwell. Accidents like this can happen."

"They shouldn't," he snapped before turning around and heading back through the treatment area. She followed him, heartily wishing for Doc Harris right now. The grizzled old vet had taken care of every dog she had ever owned, from her very first border collie and best friend, Sadie, whom she still had.

Doc Harris was her friend and mentor. If he had been here, he would have wrapped her in a warm hug that smelled of liniment and cherry Life Savers and promised her everything would be all right.

Dr. Ben Caldwell was nothing like Dr. Harris. He was abrasive and arrogant and she already heartily disliked him.

His eyes narrowed with surprise and displeasure when he saw she had followed him from the waiting room to the clinic area.

"This way is quicker," she explained. "I'm parked by the side door. I thought it would be easier to transport him on the stretcher from there."

He didn't say anything, only charged through the side door she indicated. She trotted after him, wondering how the Pine Gulch animal kingdom would get along without the kindness and compassion Dr. Harris had been renowned for.

Without waiting for her, he opened the door of the truck. As she watched, it was as if a different man had suddenly taken over. His harsh, set features seemed to ease and even the stiff set of his shoulders relaxed.

"Hello there," he crooned from the open vehicle door to the dog. "You've got yourself into a mess, haven't you?"

Even through his pain, Luke responded to the gentle-sounding stranger by trying hard to wag his tail. There was no room for both of them on the passenger side, so she went around to the driver's side and opened that door, intent on helping to lift the dog from there. By the time she made it that short distance, Dr. Caldwell had already slipped a transfer sheet under the dog and was gripping the edges.

His hands were big, she noticed, with a little light area of skin where a wedding ring once had been.

She knew a little about him from the gossip around town. It was hard to miss it when he was currently staying at the Cold Creek Inn—owned and operated by her sister-in-law Laura, married to Caidy's brother Taft.

Though Laura usually didn't gossip about her guests, over dinner last week her other brother, Trace—who made it his business as police chief to find out about everyone moving into Pine Gulch—had interrogated her so skillfully, Laura probably didn't realize what she had revealed.

From that conversation, Caidy had learned Ben Caldwell had two children, a girl and a boy, ages nine and five, respectively, and he had been a widower for two years.

Why on earth he had suddenly pulled up stakes to settle in a quiet town like Pine Gulch was a mystery to everyone. In her experience, people who came to this little corner of Idaho in the shadow of the Tetons were either looking for something or running away.

None of that was her business, she reminded herself. The only thing she cared about was the way he treated her dogs. Judging by how carefully he moved his hands over Luke's injuries, he appeared competent and even kind, at least to animals—something she generally considered a far more important character indicator than how a man treated other people.

"Okay, Luke. Just lie still, there's a good boy." He spoke in a low, calm voice. "We're going to move you now. Easy. Easy."

He handed the stretcher across the cab to her and then reached for the transfer sheet. "I'm going to lift him slightly and then you can slide the board under him. Slowly. Yes. That's it."

She had plenty of experience transferring injured animals. Years of experience. It bothered her to be treated as if she didn't know the first thing about this kind of emergency care, but now didn't seem the time to correct him.

Together they carried the stretcher into the emergency treatment room and set the dog gingerly down on the exam table.

She didn't like the pain in Luke's eyes. It reminded her a lot of how Lucky, her brother Taft's little beagle cross, had looked right after the car accident that had nearly killed him.

Now Lucky was happy as a pig in clover, she reminded herself. He lived with Taft and Laura and their two children at Taft's house near the mouth of Cold

Creek Canyon and thought he ruled the universe. If Lucky could survive his brush with death, she couldn't see any reason for Luke to do otherwise.

"That's a nasty puncture wound. At least an inch or two deep. I'm surprised it's not deeper."

That could be because she had managed to pull Luke to safety before Festus could finish taking his bad mood out on a helpless dog.

"What about the leg? Can you save it?"

"I'm going to have to x-ray before I can answer that. How far are you prepared to go for his care?"

It took her a moment to realize what he was asking in his blunt way. A difficult part of life as a vet was the knowledge that, although a vet might have the power to treat an animal successfully, sometimes the owner's ability—or willingness, for that matter—to pay was the ultimate decision maker.

"Whatever is necessary," she answered stiffly. "I don't care about the cost. Just do what you have to do."

He nodded, his attention still on her dog, and she wanted to think his hard expression thawed slightly, like a tiny crackle of ice on the edge of a much deeper lake.

"Regardless of what the X-ray shows, his treatment is going to take a few hours. You can go. Leave your number with Joni and I'll have her call you when I know more."

"No. I'll wait."

That surprise in his blue eyes annoyed the heck out of her. Did he think she would just abandon her dog here with a stranger for a couple of hours while she went off to have her hair done?

"Your choice."

"I can help you back here. I've...had some training

and I often helped Doc Harris. I actually worked here when I was a teenager."

If her life had gone a little more according to plan, *she* might have been the one taking over Doc Harris's clinic, though she hoped she wouldn't be as surly and unlikable as this new veterinarian.

"That won't be necessary." Dr. Caldwell dismissed all her hopes and dreams and volunteer work at the clinic as if they meant nothing. "Joni and I can handle it. If you insist on waiting, you can go ahead and have a seat in the waiting room."

What a jerk. She could push the matter. She *was* paying for the treatment here, after all. If she wanted to stay with her dog, there was nothing Dr. Ben No-Bedside-Manner Caldwell could do about it. But she didn't want to waste time and possibly jeopardize Luke's treatment.

"Fine," she muttered. She turned and pushed through the doors into the waiting room, seething with frustration.

After quickly sending a message to Ridge updating him on the situation and reminding her brother he would have to pick his daughter, Destry, up from the bus stop, she plopped onto one of the uncomfortable gray benches and grabbed a magazine off the side table.

She was leafing through it, barely even registering the headlines in her worry over her dog, when the bells on the door chimed and a little boy of about five burst through, followed a little more slowly by an older girl.

"Daaad! We're here!"

"Hush." A round, cheerful-looking woman who looked to be in her early sixties followed more slowly. "You know better than that, young man. Your father might be in the middle of a procedure."

"Can I go back and find him?" the girl asked.

"Because Joni isn't out here either, they must both be busy. He won't want to be bothered. You two sit down here and I'll go back to let him know we're here."

"I could go," the girl said a little sulkily, but she plopped onto the bench across from Caidy. Like father, like daughter, she thought. This was obviously the new vet's family, and his daughter, at least, seemed to share more than blue eyes with her father.

"Sit down," the girl ordered her brother. The boy didn't quite stick his tongue out at his sister, but it was a close one. Instead, he ignored her—probably a much worse insult, if Caidy remembered her own childhood with three pesky brothers—and wandered over to stand directly in front of Caidy.

The little boy had a widow's peak in his brown hair and huge dark-lashed blue eyes. A Caldwell trait, apparently.

"Hi." He beamed at her. "I'm Jack Caldwell. My sister's name is Ava. Who are you?"

"My name is Caidy," she answered.

"My dad's a dog doctor."

"Not just dogs," the girl corrected. "He's also a cat doctor. And sometimes even horses and cows."

"I know," Caidy answered. "That's why I'm here."

"Is your dog sick?" Jack asked her.

"In a way. He was hurt on our ranch. Your dad is working on him now."

"He's really good," the girl said with obvious pride. "I bet your dog will be just fine."

"I hope so."

"Our dog was hit by a car once and my dad fixed him and now he's all better," Jack said. "Well, except he only has three legs. His name is Tri. My dad says it's 'cause he always tries hard, even though he only has three legs."

Despite her worry, she managed a smile, more than a little charmed by the boy—and by the idea of the taciturn veterinarian showing any hint of sweetness.

"Tri means three," Ava informed her in a haughty sort of tone. "You know, like a *tri*cycle has three wheels."

"Good to know."

Before the children could say anything else, the older woman came back through the door leading out of the treatment room, her features set in a rueful smile.

"Looks like we're on our own for dinner, kids. Your dad is busy fixing an injured dog and he's going to be a while. We'll just go catch some dinner and then head back to the hotel for homework and bed."

"You're staying at the Cold Creek Inn, aren't you?" Caidy asked.

The other woman looked a bit wary as she nodded. "I'm sorry. Have we met?"

"I'm Caidy Bowman. My sister-in-law Laura runs the inn."

"You're Chief Bowman's sister?" There was a definite warmth in the woman's voice now, Caidy noticed wryly. Her charmer of a brother often had that effect on those of the female persuasion, no matter their age.

"I am. Both Chief Bowmans." With one brother who was the police chief and the other who headed up the fire department, not much exciting happened in town without someone in her family being in the thick of it.

"How nice to meet you. I'm Anne Michaels. I'm Dr. Caldwell's housekeeper. Or I will be when he finally gets into his house. With the maids at the inn cleaning our rooms for us, there's not much for me to do in that department. Right now I'm just the nanny, I suppose."

"Oh?"

The woman apparently didn't need any more encouragement than that simple syllable. "Dr. Caldwell is building a house on Cold Creek Road. He was supposed to close on it last week, but the contractor ran into some problems and here we are, still staying at the inn. Which is lovely, don't get me wrong, but it's still a hotel. After three weeks, all of us are a little tired of it. And now it looks like we'll be there until after the New Year. Christmas in a hotel. Can you imagine such a thing?"

Maybe that explained the man's grouchiness. She felt a little pang of sympathy, then she remembered how he had basically shoved her out of the treatment area. No, he was probably born with that temperament. He and Festus would get along just fine.

"It must be very frustrating for all of you."

"You don't know the half of it. Two children in a hotel, even a couple of rooms, for all those weeks is just too much. They need space to run. All children do. Why, in San Jose, the children had a huge backyard, complete with a pool and a swing set that rivaled the equipment at the nearest park."

"Is that where you're from, then? California?"

Anne Michaels nodded and Caidy thought she saw a note of wistfulness in the woman's eyes that didn't bode well for the chances of Dr. Caldwell's housekeeper-slash-nanny sticking around in Pine Gulch.

Anne watched the children, who were paying them no heed as they played a game on an electronic device Ava had pulled out of her backpack.

"Yes. I'm from California, born and bred. Not Dr. Caldwell. He's from back East. Chicago way. But he left everything without a backward look to head west for veterinary school at UC-Davis and that's where he met the late Mrs. Caldwell. They hired me to help out around the house when she was pregnant with little Jack there and I've been with them ever since. Those poor children needed me more than ever after their mother died. Dr. Caldwell too. That was a terrible time, I tell you."

"I'm sure."

"When he decided to move here to Idaho, he gave me the option of leaving his employment with a glowing recommendation, but I just couldn't do it. I love those children, you know?"

Caidy could relate. She loved her niece Destry as fiercely as if the girl were her own. Stepping in to help raise her after her mother walked out on Ridge and their daughter had created a powerful bond between them as unshakable as the Tetons.

"I'm sure you do."

Anne Michaels gave a rueful shake of her head. "Look at me, going on to a perfect stranger. Staying at that hotel all these weeks is making me batty!"

"Perhaps you could find a temporary rental situation until the house is finished," she suggested.

"That's what I wanted to do but Ben doesn't think we can find anyone willing to rent us a place for only a few weeks, especially over the holidays."

Caidy thought of the foreman's cottage, empty for the past six months since the young married couple Ridge had hired to help around the ranch had moved on to take a job at a Texas ranch.

It was furnished with three bedrooms and would probably fit the Caldwells' needs perfectly, but she was hesitant to mention it. She didn't like the man. Why on earth would she want him living only a quarter mile away?

"I could ask around for you if you'd like. We have a few vacation rentals in town that might be available. At least it might give you a little breathing space over the holidays until the house is finished."

"How kind you are!" Mrs. Michaels exclaimed.

A fine guilt pinched at her. If she were truly kind, she would immediately offer the foreman's cottage.

"Everyone here in Pine Gulch has been so nice and welcoming to us," the woman went on.

"I hope you feel at home here."

Again that wistfulness drifted across the woman's features like an autumn leaf tossed by the breeze, but she blinked it away. "I'm guessing the dog Dr. Caldwell is working on back there is yours, then."

Caidy nodded. "He had a run-in with a bull. When you pit a forty-pound dog against a ton of beef, the bull usually wins."

She should be back there with him. Darn it. If she were better at handling confrontations, she would have told Dr. Arrogant that she wasn't going anywhere. Instead, she was sitting out here fretting.

"He's a wonderful veterinarian, my dear. I'm sure your pet will be better before you know it."

The border collies at the River Bow Ranch weren't exactly pets—they were a vital part of the workload. Except for Sadie, anyway, who was too old to work the cattle anymore. She didn't bother to correct the woman, nor did she express any of her own doubts about the new veterinarian's competence.

"I'm hungry, Mrs. Michaels. When are we going to eat?" Bored with the game apparently, Jack had wandered back to them.

"I think your father is going to be busy for a while yet. Why don't you and Ava and I go find something? Perhaps dinner at the café tonight would be fun and we can pick something up for your father for later."

"Can I have one of the sweet rolls?" he asked, his eyes lighting up as if it were already Christmas morning.

The housekeeper laughed. "We'll have to see about that. I'd say the café's business in sweet rolls has tripled since we came to town, thanks to you alone."

"They are delish," Caidy agreed, smiling at the very cute boy.

Mrs. Michaels rose to her feet with a creak and a pop of some joint. "It was lovely to meet you, Caidy Bowman."

"I'm happy to meet you too. And I'll keep my eye out for a suitable vacation rental."

"You'll need to take that up with Dr. Caldwell, but thank you."

The woman seemed to be efficient, Caidy thought as she watched her herd the children out the door.

The reception room seemed even more bleak and colorless after the trio left. Though it was just past six, the night was already dark on this, one of the shortest days of the year. Caidy fidgeted, leafing aimlessly through her magazine for a few moments longer, then finally closed it with a rustle of pages and tossed it back onto the pile.

Darn it. That was her dog back there. She couldn't sit out here doing nothing. At the very least she deserved to know what was going on. She gathered her courage, took a deep breath and pushed through the door.

Chapter Two

Ben made the last stitch to close the incision on the puncture wound, his head throbbing and his shoulders tight from the long day that had started with an emergency call to treat an ailing horse at four in the morning.

He would have loved a nice evening with his kids and then a few hours of zone-out time watching basketball on the hotel television set. Even if he had to turn the sound low so he didn't wake up Jack, the idea sounded heavenly.

The past week had been a rough one, busy and demanding. This was what he wanted, he reminded himself. Even though the workload was heavy, he finally had the chance to build his own practice, to forge new relationships and become part of a community.

"There. That should do it for now."

"What a mess. After seeing how close that puncture

wound was to the liver, I can't believe he survived," Joni said.

He didn't want to admit to his assistant—who, after three weeks, still seemed to approve of the job he was doing—that the dog's condition was still touch and go.

"I think he's going to make it," she went on, ever the optimist. "Unlike that poor Newfoundland earlier."

All his frustration of earlier in the afternoon came surging back as he began dressing the wound. A tragedy, that was. The beautiful dog had jumped out of the back of a moving pickup truck and been hit by the car driving behind it.

That dog hadn't been as lucky as Luke here. Her injuries were just too severe and she had died on this very treatment table.

What had really pissed him off had been the attitude of the owner, more concerned at the loss of all the money he had invested in the animal than in the loss of life.

"Neither accident would have happened if not for irresponsible owners."

Joni, busy cleaning up the inevitable mess he always left behind during a surgery, looked a little surprised at his vehemence.

"I agree when it comes to Artie Palmer. He's an idiot who should have his privileges to own any animals revoked. But not Caidy Bowman. She's the last one I would call an irresponsible owner. She trains dogs and horses at the River Bow. Nobody around here does a better job."

"She didn't train this one very well, did she, if he was running wild and tangled with a bull?"

"Apparently not."

He turned at the new voice and found the dog's

owner standing in the doorway from the reception area, her lovely features taut. He swore under his breath. He meant what he said, but he supposed it didn't need to be said to *her*.

"I thought I suggested you wait in the other room."

"A suggestion? Is that what you city vets call that?" She shrugged. "I'm not particularly good at doing as I'm told, Dr. Caldwell."

Sometime during the process of caring for her dog, Ben had come to the uncomfortable realization that he had acted like a jerk to her. He never insisted owners wait outside the treatment room unless he thought they might have weak stomachs. So why had he changed policy for Caidy Bowman?

Something about her made him a little nervous. He couldn't quite put a finger on it, but it might have something to do with those impossibly green eyes and the sweet little tilt to her mouth.

"We just finished. I was about to call you back."

"I'm glad I finally disregarded your strongly worded *suggestion,* then. May I?"

He gestured agreement and she approached the table, where the dog was still working off the effects of the anesthesia.

"There's my brave boy. Oh, Luke." She smoothed a hand over the dog's head. The dog's eyes opened slightly then closed again and his breathing slowed, as if he could rest comfortably now, knowing she was near.

"It will probably take another half hour or so for the rest of the anesthesia to wear off and then we'll have to keep him here, at least overnight."

"Will someone stay with him?"

At his practice in San Jose, he and a technician would alternate stopping in every few hours through the night when they had very ill dogs staying at the clinic, but he hadn't had time yet to get fully staffed.

He nodded, watching his plans for a nice steak dinner and a basketball game in the hotel room go up in smoke. He had become pretty used to the cot in his office lately. Whatever would he do without Mrs. Michaels?

"Someone will be here with him. Don't worry about that."

A look of surprise flickered in her eyes. He couldn't figure out why for a moment, until he realized she was reacting to his soft tone. He really must have been a jackass to her.

"I'm sorry about…earlier." Apologies didn't come easily. He could probably thank his stiff, humorless grandfather for that, but this one seemed necessary. "About not letting you come in during the treatment, I mean. I should have. And about what I said just now. I'm usually not so…harsh. It's been a particularly hard day and I'm afraid I may have been taking it out on you."

She blinked a little but concealed her emotions behind an impassive look. For some reason, that made him feel even more like an idiot, a sensation he didn't like at all.

"You were able to save his leg. I thought for sure you would have to amputate."

"He wouldn't be much use as a ranch dog, then, would he?"

Her look was as cool as the December night. "Probably not. Isn't it a good thing that's not the only thing that matters to me?"

So she wasn't like his previous client, who hadn't cared about his injured dog—only dollars and cents.

"I was able to pin the leg for now, but there's no guarantee it will heal properly. We still might have to take it. He was lucky, if you want the truth. Insanely lucky. I don't know how he made it through a run-in with a bull in one piece. His injuries could have been much worse."

"What about where he was gored?"

"The bull missed all vital organs. The puncture wound is only a couple inches deep. I guess the bull wasn't that serious."

"You would think otherwise if you had been there. He definitely was seeing red. After I pulled the dog out, he rammed the fence so hard he knocked one of the poles out of its foundation."

She pulled the dog out? Crazy woman, to mess with a bull on a rampage. What was she thinking?

"Looks like he's coming around," he said, not about to enter that particular fray.

The dog whimpered and Caidy Bowman leaned down, her dark hair almost a match to the dog's coat. "Hey there. You're in a fix now, aren't you, Luke-my-boy. You'll be all right. I know it hurts now and you're confused and scared but Dr. Caldwell fixed you up and before you know it you'll be running around the ranch with King and Sadie and all the others."

Though he had paperwork to complete, he couldn't seem to wrench himself away. He stood watching her interact with the dog and winced to himself at how quickly he had misjudged her. By the gentleness of her tone and the comforting way she smoothed a hand over his fur, it was obvious the woman cared about her animal and was not inexperienced with injuries.

Next time maybe he wouldn't be quick to make surly comments when he was having a miserable day.

She smelled delicious, like vanilla splashed on wild-flowers. The scent of her drifted to him, a bright counterpoint to the sometimes unpleasant smells of a busy veterinary clinic.

It was an unsettling discovery. He didn't want to notice anything about her. Not the sweet way she smelled or the elegant curve of her neck or how, when she tucked her hair behind her ear, she unveiled a tiny beauty mark just below the lobe…

He caught the direction of his thoughts and shut them down, appalled at himself. He forced himself to move away and block the sound of her low voice crooning to the dog.

He had almost forgotten about his technician until she came out of the employee changing room, shoving her arms through the sleeves of her parka. "Do you mind if I go? I'm sorry. It's just past six-thirty and I'm supposed to be at my Bible study Christmas party in half an hour and I still have to run home and pick up my cookies for the swap."

"No. Get out of here. I'm sorry I kept you late."

"Wasn't your fault."

"Blame my curious dog," Caidy said with an apologetic smile that didn't mask the concern in her eyes.

Joni shrugged. "Accidents happen, especially on a ranch."

Ben felt another twist of guilt. She was right. Even the most careful pet owner couldn't prevent everything.

"Thanks, Ben. You both have a good night," Joni said.

"I'll walk you out," he said.

She rolled her eyes—this was an argument they had been having since he arrived. His clinic in San Jose hadn't been in the best part of the city and he would always make sure the women who worked for him made it safely to their cars in the parking lot.

It was probably an old-fashioned habit, but when he had been in vet school, a fellow student and friend had been assaulted on the way to her car after a late-night class and had ended up dropping out of school.

The cold air outside the clinic blew a little bit of energy into him. The snow of earlier had slowed to just a few flurries. The few houses around his clinic blinked their cheerful holiday lights and he regretted again that he hadn't strung a few strands in the window of the clinic.

Joni's SUV was covered in snow and he helped her brush it off.

"Thank you, Dr. Caldwell," Joni said with a smile. "You're the only employer I've ever had who scrapes my windows."

"I don't know what I'd do without you right now," he said truthfully. "I just don't want you getting into an accident on the way home."

"Thanks. Have a good night. Call me if you need me to spell you during the night."

He nodded and waved her off, then returned to the office invigorated from the cold air. He pulled open the door and caught the incongruous notes of a soft melody.

Caidy was humming, he realized. He paused to listen and it took just a moment for him to recognize the tune as "Greensleeves." He was afraid to move, not wanting to intrude on the moment. The notes seemed to seep through him, sweet and pure and somehow peaceful amid the harsh lights and complicated equipment of the clinic.

Judging by her humming, he would guess Caidy Bowman had a lovely voice.

He didn't think he had made a sound, but she somehow sensed him anyway. She looked up and a delicate pink flush washed over her cheeks. "Sorry. You must think I'm ridiculous, humming to a dog. He started to get agitated and…it seemed to calm him."

No surprise there. The melody had done the same to *him*. "Looks like he's sleeping again. I can take things from here if you need to go."

She looked uncertain. "I could stay. My brother and niece can handle chores tonight for the rest of my animals."

"We've got this covered. Don't worry. He'll be well taken care of, Ms. Bowman."

"Just Caidy. Please. No one calls me Ms. anything."

"Caidy, then."

"Is someone coming to relieve you?"

"I'm not fully staffed yet and Joni has her party tonight and then her husband and kids to get back to. No big deal. I have a cot in my office. I should be fine. When we have overnight emergency cases, I make do there."

He had again succeeded in surprising her, he saw.

"What about your children?" she asked.

"They'll be fine with Mrs. Michaels. It's only for a night."

"I… Thank you."

"You'll have a hefty bill for overnight care," he warned.

"I expected it. I worked here a decade ago and know how much things used to cost—and I've seen those charges go up in the years since." She paused. "I hate to leave him."

"He'll be fine. Don't worry. Come on. I'll walk you out."

"Is that a service you provide for every female who comes through your office?"

Close enough. "I need to lock up anyway."

She gathered her coat and shrugged into it, and then he led her back the way he had just come. The moon was filtering through the clouds, painting lovely patterns of pale light on the new snow.

Caidy Bowman drove a well-used late-model pickup truck with a king cab that was covered in mud. Bales of hay were stacked two high in the back.

"Be careful. The roads are likely to be slick after the snows of earlier."

"I've been driving these roads since before I turned sixteen. I can handle a little snow."

"I'm sure you can. I just don't want you to be the next one in need of stitching."

"Not much chance of that, but thank you for your concern. And for all you've done today. I'm sorry you won't see much of your children."

"The clinic is closed tomorrow. I can spend the whole day with them. I suppose we'll have to go look for a temporary furnished house somewhere or I'm going to have a mutiny on my hands from Mrs. Michaels, which would be a nightmare."

She opened her mouth, then closed it again, and he had the distinct impression she was waging some internal debate. Her gaze shifted to the door they had just exited through and back to him, then she drew in a breath.

"We have an empty foreman's cottage on the River Bow where you could stay."

The words spilled out of her, almost as if she had been trying to hold them back. He barely noticed, stunned by the offer.

"It's nothing fancy but it's fully furnished," she went on quickly. "It does only have three bedrooms, but if you took one and Mrs. Michaels took the other, the children could share."

"Whoa. Hold on. How do you know Mrs. Michaels? And who told you we might be looking for a place?"

"We met in the waiting room earlier. I knew you were staying at the inn because my sister-in-law Laura runs it."

If not for that moment of sweetness when he had found her humming a soothing song to her dog, he would have had a tough time believing the warm and welcoming innkeeper could be any relation to this prickly woman.

"Anyway, your housekeeper mentioned you might be looking for a place. I, uh, immediately thought of the foreman's cottage on our ranch. Nobody's using it right now, though I do try to stop in once a week or so to keep the dust down. Like I said, it's not much."

"We could manage. Are you certain?"

"I'll have to ask my brother first. Though all four of us share ownership of the ranch, Ridge is really the one in charge. I don't think he'll say no, though. Why would he?"

He didn't understand this woman. He had been extraordinarily rude to her, yet she was offering to help solve all his domestic problems in one fell swoop.

"I'm astonished, Ms. Bowman. Er, Caidy. Why would you make such an offer to a complete stranger?"

"You saved my dog," she said simply. "Besides that, I liked Mrs. Michaels and I gather she's had enough of hotel living. And how will St. Nick find your children in a hotel, as lovely as the Cold Creek Inn might be these days? They should have a proper house for the holidays, where they can play."

"I agree. That was the plan all along, but circumstances haven't exactly cooperated."

He had planned to spend the entire next day looking around for somewhere that better met their needs. He never expected the answer would fall right in his lap. A less cynical man might even call it a Christmas miracle.

"I still have to talk to Ridge. I can let you know his answer in the morning when I come to check on Luke."

"Thank you."

She gave him a hesitant smile just as the moonlight shifted. The light combined with her smile managed to transform her features from pretty to extraordinarily beautiful.

"Good night. Thank you again for your hard work."

"You're welcome."

He watched her drive away, her headlights cutting through the darkness. When he had agreed to buy James Harris's practice, he had been seeking a quiet, easy community to raise his family, a place where they could settle in and become part of things.

Pine Gulch had already provided a few more surprises than he expected—and he suddenly suspected Caidy Bowman might be one more.

Chapter Three

"You say the new vet only needs a place to stay for a few weeks?"

Caidy nodded at her oldest brother, who stood at the sink loading his and Destry's supper dishes into the dishwasher. "That's my understanding. He's building a new house on Cold Creek Road. I'm guessing it's in that new development near Taft's place. Apparently, it was supposed to be finished before he took the job, but it's behind schedule. Now it won't be ready until after Christmas."

"That's a nice area. Heck of a view. I imagine his house is probably a good sight better than our foreman's cottage."

"They're at the inn now. I got the impression the children and the housekeeper might be going a little stir-crazy there."

Ridge straightened and gave her a look she recognized well. It was his patented *What were you thinking?* look. He was ten years older than she was and she loved him dearly. He had stepped in after their parents died and had raised her for the last few years of high school and she would never be able to repay him for being her rock, even when his own marriage was faltering. He was tough and hard on the outside and sweet as could be underneath all the layers.

He still drove her crazy sometimes.

"You ever stop to think that Laura might not be too thrilled if you go around finding other lodging arrangements for her paying guests?"

"I called her already and she was cool with it. I know it's lost business, but all I had to do was paint the mental picture of Alex and Maya cooped up in a couple of hotel rooms for weeks on end—including through Christmas—and she had complete sympathy for Dr. Caldwell and his housekeeper. She thought it was a great idea."

She didn't bother telling her brother that Taft's wife had also dropped a couple of matchmaking hints a mile wide about how gorgeous the new vet was. He was kind to animals and he loved his kids. What more did she need? Laura had implied.

Ridge didn't need to know that. Much as she loved both of her sisters-in-law and considered Laura and Becca perfect for each respective twin, she didn't need her brothers joining in and trying to look around for prospective partners for her. The very idea of what they might come up with gave her chills.

After one of his long, thoughtful pauses, Ridge finally nodded. "Can't see any harm in Dr. Caldwell and his family moving in for a few weeks. The house is only sitting there empty. I can run the tractor down the lane to make sure it's cleared up for them. It might need the cobwebs swept and a little airing out."

"I'll take care of everything tomorrow after I check on Luke."

So it was settled, then. She had to fight the urge to give a giant, cartoon-style gulp. What had she just gotten herself into? She didn't want the man here.

Okay, he had been a little less like a jackass toward the end of her visit to the clinic with Luke, but that didn't mean she was obligated to invite him to move in down the road, for Pete's sake.

She still wasn't quite sure what had motivated her offer. Maybe that little spark of compassion in his blue eyes when he had tended to Luke with that surprising gentleness. Or maybe it was simply that she couldn't resist his cute son's charm.

Whatever the reason, they would only be there a few weeks. She likely wouldn't even see the man, especially as it appeared he spent most of his time at the veterinary clinic. And she could be comfortable knowing she had done her good deed for the day. Wasn't Christmas the perfect time for a little welcoming generosity?

"What did you think of his doctoring?" Ridge asked.

She thought of Luke and his carefully bandaged injuries. "He's not Doc Harris but I suppose he'll do."

Ridge chuckled. "You'll never think anybody is as good as Doc Harris. The two of you have taken care of a lot of animals together."

She had loved working at the vet clinic when she was in high school. It was just about the only thing that had kept her going after her parents died, those quiet moments when she would be holding a sick or injured animal and feeling some measure of peace.

"He's a good man. Dr. Caldwell has some pretty big boots to fill," she answered.

"From rumors I've been hearing around town, he's doing a good job of it so far."

She didn't want to talk about the veterinarian anymore. It was bad enough she couldn't seem to think about anything else since she had left the clinic.

"What were you saying to Destry after I started clearing the dishes? I heard something about the wagon," Caidy said.

He glanced through the open doorway into the dining room, where Destry was bent over the table working on a homework assignment about holiday traditions in Europe.

"Des asked me if she could invite Gabi and a couple of their other friends over for a wagon ride Sunday night. She suggested caroling to the neighbors."

She never should have shared with Destry her memories of doing that very thing with their parents when she and the boys were young. "What did you tell her?"

He didn't answer, but he didn't need to. She could tell by his expression that he had given in. Ridge might be a hard man when it came to their cattle and the ranch, but when it came to his daughter he was soft as new taffy.

"You're a good father, Ridge."

"She loves Christmas," he finally said. "What can I do?"

The rest of them weren't quite as fond of the holidays as Des but they put on a good show for her sake. Since their parents' murders just a few days before Christmas eleven years ago, the holidays seemed to dredge up difficult emotions.

Becca and Laura had worked some kind of sparkly holiday magic over Trace and Taft. This year the twins seemed to be more into the spirit of Christmas than she'd ever seen them. They had both volunteered to cut trees for everyone. They had even gone a little overboard, cutting a few extras for neighbors and friends.

She and Ridge didn't share their enthusiasm, though they both went through the motions every year. Caidy even had all her Christmas presents wrapped and the actual holiday was still more than a week away. No more last-minute panics for her this year.

"What time are they coming?"

"I told her to make arrangements for about seven. I figured we would be done with Sunday dinner by then."

Though Taft and Trace both lived closer to town, her brothers usually brought their families out to the ranch every week. With the hectic pace of their lives protecting and serving the good people of Pine Gulch, it was sometimes the only chance she had to see them all week.

"I'll throw some cookies in just before they get here so they can have something warm in their little bellies before they go. And I'll make hot chocolate for the ride, of course."

"Thanks. Destry will appreciate that, I'm sure." He finished wiping down the countertop and set the cloth on the sink's edge. "You won't consider coming with us?"

By his solemn expression, she knew he was aware just what he asked of her. "I don't think so."

"You would really send me off on my own with five or six giggly girls?"

"You can take one of the dogs with you," she offered with a grin.

He made a face but quickly grew serious again. "It's been eleven years, Caidy. Taft and Trace have moved on and both have families. Of all of us, you deserve to do the same. I wish you could find a little Christmas joy again."

"I find plenty of joy the rest of the year. Just not so much in December."

His mouth tightened, his eyes darkening with familiar sadness. Each of them had struggled in different ways after their parents' deaths. Ridge had become more stoic and controlled, Taft had gone a little crazy dating all the wild women at the tavern in town and Trace had become a dedicated lawman.

And she was still hiding away here at the River Bow.

"You need to move on," her brother said. "Maybe it's time you think about trying school again."

"Maybe." She gave a noncommittal answer, too tired to fight with him right now after the ordeal of Luke's injury and the hours spent in the waiting room of the veterinary clinic. "Hey, thanks again for letting the vet stay in the foreman's cottage. It shouldn't be longer than a few weeks."

Ridge wasn't fooled for a moment. He knew she was trying to change the subject. For once he didn't try to call her on it.

"Just think. For a few weeks anyway we'll have our own veterinarian-in-residence. With your menagerie, that should come in pretty handy."

She made a face. Given her unwilling reaction to the man, she would rather not have need of his professional services again anytime soon.

A good four inches of snow fell during the night. It clung to the trees and bowed down the branches, turning the town into an enchanting winter wonderland, especially with the craggy mountains looming in the distance.

Added to the few inches that had fallen the previous evening, that should be plenty for Destry to have a great time with her friends on the sleigh ride the next night, Caidy thought as she drove through the quiet stillness of the unplowed roads on her way to the clinic the next morning.

It wasn't yet seven. She hadn't slept well, her dreams a troubled, tangled mess. With worry for Luke uppermost in her mind, she had risen early and finished her chores. Ridge could take care of breakfast for him and Destry when he finished his own chores. Saturday morning pancakes were his specialty.

Even with her restless sleep, she could appreciate the beauty of the morning. Colorful Christmas trees gleamed in the windows of a few houses, and she liked to imagine the children there rushing to plug in the lights the moment they woke up so they could enjoy the display before the sun was fully up.

When she reached Dr. Caldwell's office, she wasn't particularly surprised to see the parking lot hadn't been plowed yet. Like many of the small businesses in Pine Gulch, he probably paid a service to take care of that for him and the plows hadn't made it here yet.

With four-wheel drive and high clearance, her truck had no problem navigating through the snow. Mindful of helping the plow work around her vehicle, she parked at the edge of the lot, next to a snow-covered Range Rover she assumed must belong to Ben.

As she headed for the building, she worried she might be waking him after a long night of watching over Luke. The sidewalks had been cleared, though. Unless he paid someone else to take care of that chore, she guessed Ben had taken care of the shoveling himself.

She wasn't surprised to find the front door locked. When Doc Harris was here, she never had to bother with the front door; she could use the side entrance she had used the night before.

Likely that's where she would find Ben Caldwell. She trudged through the snow, enjoying the brisk cold and the scent of snowy pine. A couple hard raps on the door elicited no response. She checked the door and the knob turned easily in her hand.

After a quick internal debate, she turned the knob and stepped inside. She opened her mouth to call out a greeting but the words vanished somewhere in the vicinity of her tongue—along with any remaining air in her lungs—at the sight of the new veterinarian coming out of the locker room wearing only jeans and toweling off his wet hair.

That dramatic cartoon gulp sounded in her head again. Wow. Double wow. With ice cream on top.

His chest was broad and well-defined with solid muscle and a little line of hair arrowed down to disappear in the waistband of his Levi's, where he hadn't yet fastened the top button.

Awareness bloomed inside her, as bright and vivid as the always unexpected crocuses that popped up through the snow along the fenceline of the River Bow every spring.

Her toes tingled and her heartbeat kicked up a notch and she wanted to stand here for the next few years and just stare.

He continued toweling his hair, oblivious to her, biceps flexing with the motion, and she completely forgot about the reason she had come. Suddenly he dropped the towel and saw her standing there.

His pupils widened and for a long moment, he returned her stare. Tension seethed between them, writhing and alive. Her insides trembled and every thought in her head seemed scrambled and incoherent.

Finally he cleared his throat. "Oh. Hi. I didn't hear you come in."

"Sorry." Her voice sounded raspy and she quickly cleared it, mortified that he had caught her gaping at him like Destry and her friends at a Justin Bieber concert. "I knocked and was just checking the door and it opened and…there you were."

Could she sound any more stupid? Good grief. She wanted to slink away through the door and bury her face in a pile of snow somewhere. Anybody might think she'd never seen a gorgeous, half-naked man before.

"I just… I can go and come back, uh, later."

"Why?" He grabbed a clean scrub top and she couldn't seem to look away as he pulled it over that delicious chest, her gaze fixed on the disappearance of that little strip of hair trailing down his abdomen.

Despite his towel job, his hair was still wet and sticking up in spikes. He made an effort to smooth it down but only ended up making it look more tousled and sexy.

She wanted to gulp again, feeling very much like some ridiculous maiden aunt.

Which she was.

"I shouldn't have come so early. I was just…concerned about how you made it through the night."

He shrugged, though she thought she noticed a little spark of *something* in the depths of his blue eyes. "Not too badly. Luke slept most of the night. I imagine he's going to be ready for a walk around the yard soon."

That must have been why he had cleared away the snow around the sidewalk. She had wondered why that had been a priority, especially because he had told her the clinic would be closed that day.

She fought the little burst of warmth in her chest. *Get a grip,* she told herself. She wasn't interested in some prickly veterinarian who jumped to conclusions and made snap judgments about people before he knew the facts.

Even if he did have a flat stomach she wanted to trail her fingers along...

She blushed and looked away. Her dog. That's why she was here—to check on Luke. Not to engage in completely inappropriate fantasies about a man who would be living just a stone's throw away from her.

"I can take him out if you're sure he's up to it."

"We made one trip out in the night. He seemed to handle it okay. Let's try again."

She headed to the crate where Luke lay. As if sensing her presence, his eyes opened and he tried to wag his tail, which just about broke her heart. "Shhh. Easy. Easy. There's my boy. How's my favorite guy?"

The dog's black tail flapped again on the soft blankets inside the crate. He tried to scramble up, then subsided again with a whimper.

"He's due for pain meds again. I was planning to try to slip a pill in some peanut butter."

She unlatched the door of the crate and reached in to rub his chin. "I hope you didn't keep Dr. Caldwell up all night."

"Not too bad." Ben hadn't shaved yet and the dark shadow along his jawline gave him a rugged, rather disreputable air. He probably wouldn't appreciate her pointing that out—and he *definitely* wouldn't be interested in knowing about her unwilling attraction to him.

"We had a few rough moments." He paused, giving her a careful look. "To tell the truth, I wasn't completely convinced he would make it through the night. He's a tough little guy."

"It helps to have a good vet," she said. Even Doc Harris wouldn't have stayed all night. It was a hard admission, but honesty compelled her to face it. As much as she loved the old veterinarian, she had noticed he sometimes had a bit of a cavalier attitude about the seriousness of some cases.

Apparently that wasn't the case with Dr. Caldwell.

"Sometimes all the veterinarian skills in the world aren't enough. I guess you would know that, as an animal lover."

That was her big worry right now with Sadie. Her old border collie, the very first dog who had been only hers, was thirteen. In border collie terms, that was ancient. As much as she loved her, Caidy knew she wouldn't be around forever.

"Luke seems alert now. That's a good sign, isn't it?"

He joined her in petting the dog. Their fingers accidentally touched and she didn't miss the way he quickly lifted his hands. "You can call him Lucky Luke."

"My brother and his family already have a dog named Lucky Lou," she said with a smile. "He survived being hit by a car."

"Your brother?"

She rolled her eyes. "No, but there was a time plenty of the scorned women of Pine Gulch would have gladly tried to run him down. No, Lou. He was a stray, a little corgi-beagle mix who used to wander around our ranch. I was trying to lure him in so I could find his owner, but he was pretty skittish. Then one afternoon he didn't move fast enough and some speeder hit him. He's doing great now and is extremely spoiled by Taft's kids."

Stepchildren, actually, but Maya and Alex had quickly been absorbed into the Bowman clan.

"Well, you can add this one to your collection of lucky pups."

"When can I take him home?"

"Maybe later today, as long as he remains stable."

"That would be great. Thank you for everything."

He shrugged. "It's my job."

She owed him now. It was an uncomfortable realization—she didn't like being beholden to anyone, especially not very attractive veterinarians.

In this case, she could even the playing field a little bit. "I talked to Ridge last night. He says you and your family are more than welcome to move into the foreman's cottage until your house is finished."

"Did he?" he asked, his expression pleased and more than a little relieved. "That would make the holidays much more comfortable all the way around."

"You may want to come out to the ranch and take a look at the place before you agree. We've kept it up well, but it could probably use a remodel one of these days."

"Three bedrooms, you said?"

"Yes. And Ridge suggested we work something out with rent in trade for vet services, if you're agreeable. I'll still probably owe you my firstborn but maybe not my second."

He smiled—not a huge smile but a genuine one. Her stomach flip-flopped again and she remembered that moment when she had walked into the clinic and found him half-dressed.

What in heaven's name had come over her? She did

not react to men this way. She just didn't. Oh, she dated once in a while. She wasn't a complete hermit, contrary to what her brothers teased her about. She enjoyed the occasional dinner or movie out, but she usually worked hard to keep things casual and fun. The few times a guy had tried to push for more, she had felt panicky and pressured and had done her best to discourage him.

She couldn't remember having such an instant and powerful reaction to a man, this immediate curl of desire. She certainly wasn't used to this jittery, off-balance feeling, as if she were teetering in the loft door of the barn, gearing up to jump into the big pile of hay below.

Ridiculous. She wasn't even sure she *liked* Ben Caldwell yet. She certainly wasn't ready to jump into any pile of hay with him, literally or figuratively.

"I'm sure it's fine," he answered. "If it has three bedrooms and a halfway decent kitchen for Mrs. Michaels, I don't care about much else."

She drew in a breath and subtly shifted to ease her shoulder away from his. "For all you know, it might be a hovel. You would be surprised at the living conditions some ranchers force on their workers."

"I would like to think you wouldn't have suggested it if you didn't think it would work for my family."

"That's trusting of you. You don't know anything about me. For all you know, maybe I make it a habit of bilking unsuspecting newcomers out of their rent money."

"Since we're talking about trading veterinary services for rent, that's not an issue, is it? But if you insist, I guess I could stop by your ranch later this morning after Joni comes in to relieve me. She's coming in around ten."

"That should work. I should have just enough time to

rush back there and hide all the mousetraps and roach motels."

This time he laughed outright, as she had intended. It was a full, rich sound that shimmied down her spine as if he'd pressed his lips there.

This was a gigantic mistake. Why had she ever opened her big, stupid mouth about the foreman's cottage in the first place? The last thing she needed on the ranch right now was a gorgeous man with a sexy chest and a delicious laugh.

"Should I help you take Luke outside before I go?"

He seemed to know she was doing her best to change the subject. "No. I can handle it."

She nodded. "I'll see you in a bit, okay?" she said, rubbing the dog's head again. "You need to stay here just a little longer and then you can come home."

Luke whined as if he knew she were going to leave. It was tough but she shut the crate door again.

"You know he'll probably never be a working dog now. I set the bones as well as I could, but he'll never be fast enough or strong enough to do what he used to."

"We're not so cruel that we'll make him sing for his supper, Dr. Caldwell. We'll still find a place for him on the River Bow, whether he can work the cattle or not. We have plenty of other animals who live on in comfortable retirement."

"I'm glad to hear that," he answered.

She firmly ignored his disreputable smile and the jumping nerves it set off in her stomach.

"Thanks again for everything. I guess I'll see you later."

She headed to the door, but to her dismay, he beat her to it and held it open, leaving her no choice but to brush past him on her way out. She ignored the little shiver of awareness, just as she had ignored all the others.

She could do this, she told herself. It would only be for a few weeks and she likely would see far more of his housekeeper and children than she would Ben, especially if he consistently maintained these sorts of hours.

Chapter Four

"But I *like* staying at the hotel. We have Alex and Maya to play with there and someone makes breakfast for us every day. It's kind of like Eloise at the Plaza."

Ben swallowed a laugh, certain his bristly nine-year-old daughter wouldn't appreciate it. If there was one thing Ava hated worse than eating her brussels sprouts, it was being the object of someone else's amusement.

Still, as lovely as the twenty-four room Cold Creek Inn was, the place was nothing like the grand hotel in New York City portrayed in the series of books Ava adored.

"It has been fun," he conceded, "but wouldn't you like to have a little more room to play?"

"In the middle of nowhere with a bunch of cows and horses? No. Not really."

He sighed, not unfamiliar with Ava's condescending attitude. He knew just where it came from—her maternal grandparents.

Ava wasn't thrilled to be separated from his late wife's parents. She loved the Marshalls and tried to spend as much time as she could with them. For the past two years, since Brooke's death, Robert and Janet had filled Ava's head with subtle digs and sly innuendo in an ongoing campaign to undermine her relationship with her father.

The Marshalls wanted nothing more than to take over guardianship of the children any way they could.

He blamed himself for the most part. Right after Brooke's death, he had been too lost and grief-stricken to see the fissures they were carving in his relationship with his children. The first time he figured it out had been about six months ago. After an overnight stay, Jack had refused to give him a hug.

It had taken several days and much prodding on his part, but the boy had finally tearfully confessed that Grandmother Marshall told him he killed dogs and cats nobody wanted—a completely unfair accusation because he was working at a no-kill shelter at the time.

He had done his best to keep distance between them after that, but the Marshalls were insidious in their efforts to drive a wedge between them and had even gone to court seeking regular visitation with their grandchildren.

He knew he couldn't keep them away forever, but he had decided his first priority must be strengthening the bond between him and his children, and eventually he had decided his only option was to resettle elsewhere to make the interactions between them more difficult.

"It's only for a few weeks, until our house is finished," he said now to Ava. "Haven't you missed Mrs. Michaels's delicious dinners?"

"I have," Jack opined from his booster seat next to his sister. "I looove the way she makes mac and cheese."

Ben's mouth watered as he thought of the caramelized onions she scattered across her gooey macaroni and cheese.

"If we move into this new place, that will be the first thing I ask her to make," he promised Jack and was rewarded with a huge grin.

"It hasn't been bad going for dinner at the diner or having stuff from the microwave in the hotel room," Ava insisted. "I haven't minded one single bit."

He sighed. Her constant contrariness was beginning to grate on every nerve.

"What about Christmas? Do you really want to spend Christmas Eve in the hotel, where we don't even have our own tree in our rooms?"

She didn't immediately answer and he could see her trying to come up with something to combat that. Before she could, he pursued his advantage. "Let's just check it out. If we all hate it, we can stay at the hotel through the holidays. With any luck, our new house will be done by early January."

"Will I have to ride the bus to school for the last week of school before Christmas vacation?"

He hadn't thought that far ahead. He supposed he should have considered the logistics before considering this option. "You can if you want to. Or we can try to arrange our schedules so I can take you to school on my way to the clinic."

"I wouldn't want to ride a bus. It's probably totally gross."

That was another lovely gift from his late wife's parents, thank you very little. Janet Marshall had done her best to turn his daughter into a paranoid germaphobe.

"You can always use hand sanitizer." This had become his common refrain, used to combat her objections for everything from eating in a public restaurant to sitting on Santa's lap at the mall.

She sniffed but didn't have a response for that. Much to his relief, she let the subject go and subsided into one of her aggrieved silences. He had a feeling Ava was going to drive him crazy before she made it to the other side of puberty.

A few moments later, he pulled into a side road with a log arch over it that said River Bow Ranch. Pines and aspens lined the drive. Though it was well plowed, he was still grateful for his four-wheel drive as he headed up a slight hill toward the main log ranch house he could see sprawling in the distance.

Not far from the house, the drive forked. About a city block down it, he saw a smaller clapboard home with two small eaves above a wide front porch.

He couldn't help thinking it looked like something off of one of the Christmas cards the clinic had received, a charming little house nestled in the snow-topped pines, with split rail fencing on the pastures that lined the road leading up to it.

"Can we ride the horses while we're here?" Jack asked, gazing with excitement at a group of about six or seven that stood in the snow eating a few bales of alfalfa that looked as though they had recently been dropped into the pasture.

"Probably not. We're only renting a house, not the whole ranch."

Ava looked out the window at the horses too, and he didn't miss the sudden light in her eyes. She loved horses, just like most nine-year-old girls.

But even the presence of some beautiful horseflesh

wasn't enough. "You said we were only looking at it and if we didn't like it, we didn't have to stay," she said in an accusatory tone.

Oh, she made him tired sometimes.

"Yes. That's what I said."

"I like it," Jack offered with his unassailable kindergarten logic. "They have dogs and horses and cows."

A couple of collies that looked very much like the one currently resting in his clinic watched them from the front porch of the main house as he pulled into the circular drive in front.

Before he could figure out what to do next, the door opened and Caidy Bowman trotted down the porch steps, pulling on a parka. She must have been watching for them, he thought. The long driveway would certainly give advance notice of anybody approaching.

She wore her dark hair in a braid down her back, topped with a tan Stetson. She looked rather sweet and uncomplicated, but somehow he knew the reality of Caidy Bowman was more tangled than her deceptively simple appearance would indicate.

He opened his door and climbed out as she approached his vehicle.

"The house is just there." She gestured toward the small farmhouse in the trees. "Why don't you drive closer so you don't have to walk through the snow? Ridge plowed it out with the tractor this morning so you shouldn't have any trouble. I'll just meet you there."

"Why?" He went around the vehicle and opened the passenger door. "Get in. We can ride together."

For some reason she looked reluctant at that idea, but after a weird little pause, she finally came to where he was standing and jumped up into the vehicle. He closed the door behind her before she could change her mind.

The first thing he noticed after he was once more behind the wheel was the scent of her filling the interior. Though it was a cold and overcast December day, his car suddenly smelled of vanilla and rain-washed wildflowers on a mountain meadow somewhere.

He was aware of a completely inappropriate desire to inhale that scent deep inside him, to sit here in his car with his children in the backseat and just savor the sweetness.

Get a grip, Caldwell, he told himself. So she smelled good. He could walk into any perfume counter in town and probably get the same little kick in his gut.

Still, he was suddenly fiercely glad his house would be finished in only a few weeks. Much longer than that and he was afraid he would develop a serious thing for this prickly woman who smelled like a wild garden.

"Welcome to the River Bow Ranch."

He almost thanked her before he realized she was looking in the backseat and talking to his children. She wore a genuine smile, probably the first one he had seen on her, and she looked like a bright, beautiful ray of sunshine on an overcast day.

"Can I ride one of your horses sometime?"

"Jack," Ben chided, but Caidy only laughed.

"I think that can probably be arranged. We've got several that are very gentle for children. My favorite is Old Pete. He's about the nicest horse you could ever meet."

Jack beamed at her, his sunny, adorable self. "I bet I can ride a horse good. I have boots and everything."

"You're such a dork. Just because you have boots doesn't make you a cowboy," Ava said with an impatient snort.

"What about you, Ava? Do you like horses?"

In the rearview mirror, he didn't miss his daughter's eagerness but she quickly concealed it. He wondered sometimes if she was afraid to hope for things she wanted anymore because none of their prayers and wishes had been enough to keep Brooke alive.

"I guess," she said, picking at the sleeve of her parka.

"You've come to the right place, then. I bet my niece Destry would love to take you out for a ride."

Ava's eyes widened. "Destry from my school? She's your niece?"

Caidy smiled. "I guess so. There aren't too many Destrys in this neck of the woods. You've met her?"

Ava nodded. "She's a couple years older than me but on my very first day, Mrs. Dalton, the principal, had her show me around. She was supernice to me and she still says hi to me and stuff when she sees me at school."

"I'm very glad to hear that. She better be nice. If she's not, you let me know and I'll give her a talking-to until her ears fall off."

Jack laughed at the image. Ava looked as if she wanted to join him but she had become very good at hiding her amusement these days. Instead, she looked out the window again.

"Here we are," Caidy said when he pulled up front of the house. "I turned up the heat earlier when I came down to clean a little. It should be nice and cozy for you."

How much work had she done for them? He hoped it wasn't much, even as he wondered why she was making this effort for them when he wasn't at all sure she really wanted them there.

"So all the rattraps are gone?" he asked.

"Rats?" Ava asked in a horrified voice.

"There are no rats," Caidy assured her quickly. "We

have too many cats here at the River Bow. Your father was making a joke. Weren't you?"

Was he? It had been quite a while since he had found much to joke about. Somehow Caidy Bowman brought out a long-forgotten side of him. "Yes, Ava. I was teasing."

Judging by his daughter's expression, she seemed to find that notion just as unsettling as the idea of giant rodents in her bed.

"Shall we go inside so you can see for yourself?" Caidy said.

"I want to see the rats!" Jack said.

"There are no rats," Ben assured everybody again as Caidy pushed open the front door. It wasn't locked, he noticed—something very different from his security-conscious world in California.

The scent of pine washed over them the moment they stepped inside.

"Look!" Jack exclaimed. "A Christmas tree! A real live one of our very own!"

Sure enough, in the corner was a rather scraggly pine tree as tall as he was, covered in multicolored Christmas lights.

He gazed at it, stunned at the sight and quite certain the tree hadn't been there a few hours earlier. She had said the house was empty, so somehow in the past few hours Caidy Bowman must have dragged this tree in, set it in the stand and strung the Christmas lights.

She had done this for them. He didn't know what to say. Somewhere inside him another little chunk of ice seemed to fall away.

"You didn't need to do that," he said, a little more gruffly than he intended.

"It was no big deal," she answered. In the warmth

of the room he thought he saw a tinge of color on her cheeks. "My brothers went a little crazy in the Christmas tree department. We cut our own in the mountains above the ranch after Thanksgiving, and this year they cut a few extras to give to people who might need them. This one was leftover."

"What about the lights?"

"We had some extras lying around. I'm afraid this one is a little on the scrawny side, but paper garland and some ornaments will fix that right up. I bet your dad and Mrs. Michaels can help you make some," she told Ava and Jack. As he might have expected, Jack looked excited about the idea but Ava merely shrugged.

He wouldn't know the first thing about making ornaments for a Christmas tree. Brooke had always taken care of the holiday decorating and his housekeeper had stepped in after her death.

"Come on. I'll give you the grand tour. It's not much, as you can see. Just this room, the kitchen and dining room and the bedrooms upstairs."

She was too modest. This room alone was already half again as big as one of the hotel rooms. The living room was comfortably furnished with a burgundy plaid sofa and a couple of leather recliners, and the television set was an older model but quite large.

One side wall was dominated by a small river rock fireplace with a mantel made of rough-hewn lumber. The fireplace was empty but someone—probably Caidy—had stacked several armloads of wood in a bin next to it. He could easily imagine how cozy the place would be with a fire in the hearth, the lights flickering on the tree and a basketball game on the television set. He wouldn't even have to worry about turning the volume down so he didn't wake Jack. It was an appealing thought.

"Through here is the kitchen and dining area," she said.

The appliances looked a little out-of-date but perfectly adequate. The refrigerator even had an ice maker, something he had missed in the hotel. Ice from a bucket wasn't quite the same for some reason.

"There's a half bath and a laundry room through those doors. It's pretty basic. Do you want to see the upstairs?"

He nodded and followed her up, trying not to notice the way her jeans hugged her curves. "We've got a king bed in one room, a queen in the second bedroom and bunk beds in that one on the left. The children won't mind sharing, will they?"

"I want to see!" Jack exclaimed and raced into the room she indicated. Ava followed more slowly, but even she looked curious about the accommodations, he saw.

The whole place smelled like vanilla and pine, fresh and clean, and he didn't miss the vacuum tracks in the carpet. She really must have hurried over to make it ready for them.

"There's a small bathroom off the master and another one in the hall between the other bedrooms. That's it. Not much to it. Do you think it will work?"

"I like it!" Jack declared. "But only if I get the top bunk."

"What do you think, Ava?"

She shrugged. "It's okay. I still like the hotel better but it would be fun to live by Destry and ride the bus with her and stuff. And *I* get the top bunk. I'm older."

"We can work that out," Ben said. "I guess it's more or less unanimous. It should be great. Comfortable and spacious and not that far from the clinic. I appreciate the offer."

She smiled but he thought it looked a little strained. "Great. You can move in anytime. Today if you want. All you need are your suitcases."

The idea of a little breathing space was vastly appealing. "In that case, we can go back to the inn and pack our things and be back later this afternoon. Mrs. Michaels will be thrilled."

"That should work."

"Can we decorate the tree tonight?" Jack asked eagerly.

He tousled his son's hair, deeply grateful for this cheerful child who gave his love unconditionally. "Yeah. We can probably do that. We'll pick up some art supplies while we're in town too."

Even Ava looked mildly excited about that as they headed back outside.

"Oh, for goodness' sake," Caidy said suddenly. "What are you doing all the way down here, you crazy dog? Just want to make a few new friends, do you?"

She spoke to an ancient-looking collie, with a gray muzzle and tired eyes, that was sitting at the bottom of the porch steps. Caidy knelt down, heedless of the snow, and petted the dog. "This is Sadie. She's just about my best friend in the world."

Ava smiled at the dog. "Hi, Sadie."

Jack, however, hovered behind Ben. His son was nervous about any dog bigger than a Pekingese.

"She's really old. Thirteen. I got her when I was just a teenager. We've been through a lot, Sadie and me."

"Sadie and Caidy. That rhymes," Ava said unexpectedly, earning a giggle from Jack.

"I know, right? My brothers used to call the dog and

I would think they wanted me. Or they would call me and Sadie would come running. It was all very confusing but we're used to it now after all these years. I didn't name her, though—the rancher my parents got her from had already given her a name. By then she was already used to it so we decided not to change it."

He saw a hint of sadness in her eyes and wondered at the source of it as she hugged the dog. "Do you know, she was a Christmas present the year I turned fourteen? That's not much older than you, Ava."

His daughter looked thrilled that someone would think she was anywhere close to the advanced age of fourteen instead of nine and he suddenly knew Caidy had said it on purpose.

"For months I'd been begging and begging for a dog of my own," she went on. "We always had ranch dogs but my brothers took over working with them. I wanted one I could train myself. I was so excited that morning when I found her under the tree. She was so adorable with a big red bow around her neck."

He pictured it clearly, a teenage Caidy and a cute little border collie puppy with curious ears and a wagging tail. He could certainly relate to the story. When he had been a boy, he had begged for a dog every year from about the time he turned eight. Every year, he had hoped and prayed he would find a puppy under the tree and every year had been another disappointment.

He held the door open. "Ava, you can sit in the middle next to Jack so we can make room for Sadie."

"Oh, no. That's not necessary. She's probably wet and stinky. We can walk. It's not that far."

"If there's one thing we don't mind in this family, it's wet stinky dogs, isn't that right? Just wait until we bring Tri out here to romp in the snowdrifts."

Both children giggled, even Ava, which filled him with a great sense of accomplishment.

He turned his attention away from his children to find Caidy watching him, her hand still on her dog's scruff and an arrested expression in her eyes. He felt a return of that tensile connection of earlier, when he had walked out of the shower room to find her standing in the hallway.

The moment stretched between them and he couldn't seem to look away, vaguely aware of Jack and Ava climbing into the SUV with their usual bickering.

Finally she cleared her throat. "Thanks anyway, but I'm not quite ready to go. I just need to dust out the two spare bedrooms."

This wasn't going to work. He didn't want this sudden attraction. He didn't want to feel this heat in his gut again, the sizzle of his blood.

He thought about telling her he had changed his mind, but how ridiculous would that sound? *I can't stay here because I'm afraid I'll do something stupid if I'm in the same general vicinity of you.*

Anyway, now that he had seen the charming little house, he really didn't want to go back to the cramped quarters of the inn. He would just have to work hard to stay out of her way. How tough could that be?

"The place looked fine. We can dust," he said. "You don't have to do that."

"We Bowmans are a proud lot. Though we might not be in the landlord business as a regular thing, I'm not about to let you stay in a dirty place."

He decided not to argue. "I'll check on Luke while we're in town. If I feel like he is stable enough to be here, I'll pick him up and bring him out with us when we come back."

She smiled her gratitude and he felt that inexorable tug toward her again. "Thank you! We would love that, wouldn't we, Sadie?"

The dog nudged her hand and seemed to smile in agreement.

"Luke is her great-grandson," she explained to the children. "So I guess I'll see you all later. I'm glad the house will work for you."

Space-wise, the house was perfect. Neighbor-wise, he wasn't so sure.

After he loaded up the kids and started down the gravel drive, he glanced in the rearview mirror. Caidy Bowman was lifting her face to the pale winter sun peeking between clouds, one hand on the dog's grizzled head.

For some ridiculous reason, a lump rose in his throat at the sight and he had a hard time looking away.

Chapter Five

For the next few hours, Caidy couldn't shake a tangled mix of dread and anticipation. Offering Ben and his family a place to stay over the holidays had been a friendly, neighborly gesture. She was grateful those cute kids would be able to have the fun of sneaking downstairs Christmas morning to see their presents under their very own tree and that Mrs. Michaels could cook a proper dinner for them instead of something out of the microwave.

Even so, she had the strangest feeling that life on the ranch was about to change, maybe irrevocably.

It was only for a few weeks, she told herself as she finished mucking out the stalls with Destry while Sadie plopped on her belly in the warm straw and watched them. She could handle anything for a few weeks. Still, the strange, restless mood dogged her heels like the collies in a thunderstorm as she went through her Saturday chores.

"You ladies need a hand in here?"

Destry beamed at her father, thrilled when he called her a lady. She was, Caidy thought. Her little girl was growing up—nearly eleven now and going to middle school the next year. She didn't know what she would do then.

"Since we've got your muscles here, why don't you bring us a couple new straw bales? I'd like to put some fresh down for the foaling mares."

"Will do. Des, come give your old man a hand."

The two of them took off, laughing together about something Destry said in answer, and Caidy again felt that unaccountable depression seep over her.

Her brother didn't really need her help anymore with Destry. She had been happy to offer it when the girl was young and Ridge had been alone and struggling. *More* than happy, really. Relieved, more like, to have something useful to do with her time, something she thought she could handle.

Destry was almost a young woman now and Ridge was an excellent father who could probably handle things here just fine by himself.

She leaned her cheek on the handle of the shovel and watched Sadie snoring away. They didn't need her. Nobody did. She sighed heavily just as Ridge came back alone with a bale on each shoulder.

"That sounds serious. What's wrong? Having second thoughts about the new vet and his family moving in?"

And third and fourth. She shrugged, picked up a pitchfork and started spreading the straw around. "What's to have second thoughts about? He needed a place to stay for a few weeks and we have an empty, furnished house just sitting there."

"Destry will enjoy having other children around the ranch, especially for Christmas."

"Where is she?"

He grabbed the other pitchfork to help her. "She got distracted by the new barn kittens. She's up in the loft giving them a little attention."

Her niece loved animals every bit as much as Caidy had at her age. Maybe she would be a veterinarian someday. "I'm afraid we're not very good company for her this time of year, are we? Things will be better in January."

Ridge gave her a long look. "You remember how much Mom loved Christmas. She would hate thinking you would let her and Dad's deaths ruin the holidays forever."

"I know." It wasn't a new argument between them and right now she wasn't in the mood, not with this melancholy sidling through her. "Don't make it sound like I'm the only one. You hate Christmas too."

"Yeah, well, I think it's time we both moved forward with our lives. Taft and Trace both have."

You weren't there, she wanted to cry out. None of her brothers were. She had been the one hiding under that shelf in the pantry, listening to her mother's dying gasps and knowing there wasn't a damn thing she could do about it.

You weren't there and you weren't responsible.

She couldn't say the words to him. She never could. Instead she spread a little more straw in an area that already had plenty.

"I think it's time you went back to school."

She didn't need this again, today, of all days, when

she felt so oddly as if she were teetering on the brink of some major life shift.

"I'm twenty-seven years old, Ridge. I think my school days are past me."

Her brother's handsome features twisted into a scowl. "They don't have to be. Plenty of people finish college when they're a little older than the traditional student. Sometimes it takes a person a few years to figure out what they want out of life."

"Have I figured that out yet?" she muttered.

"You won't while you're stuck here. I should never have let you come home after your first year of college. I should have made you stick it out. Believe me, I've regretted it bitterly, more than I can say. The truth is, after Melinda walked out, I needed you here to help me with Destry. I was lost and floundering, trying to run the ranch and take care of her too."

He pulled his gloves off and shoved them in his back pocket, then tugged at an earlobe. These words weren't easy for him, she knew. Of all her brothers, Ridge was the most stoic, hiding his emotions and his thoughts behind the hard steel it took to run a ranch like the River Bow.

"The truth is, I chose the easy path instead of the right one," he said, regret in his eyes.

"You didn't choose anything. I did. I wanted to come home. I would have dropped out regardless of whether you needed me here."

"Not if I hadn't made it so easy for you to find a soft place to land back home."

She wasn't sure if her brothers blamed her for the murders of her parents. She had always been afraid to ask and none of them had ever talked about it.

How could they not blame her on some level? Neither she nor her parents were even supposed to have been home that night. That was the reason an art burglary had turned into a surprise home invasion robbery and then a double murder when her father had tried to stop the thieves.

Caidy would have died with them if her mother hadn't shoved her into the pantry and ordered her to hide.

Sometimes she felt as if she had been hiding ever since.

"*You* should be the new veterinarian in town, not some new guy from the coast," Ridge went on, his voice fierce. "It's been eating at me ever since this Caldwell showed up. Becoming a vet was all you ever wanted. I know Doc Harris had once hoped you would follow in his footsteps. I can't help thinking how, if things had gone differently, you could have taken over his practice when he retired."

He managed to hit exactly on the reason for her restlessness. The straw rustled under her feet as she shifted her boots, releasing its earthy scent. Ben Caldwell was living her dream now. It was hard to admit, especially when she knew she had absolutely no right to be upset.

"I made my choices, Ridge. I don't regret them. Not for a moment."

"You need a life of your own. A home, a family. You never even date."

"Maybe I'll just run off with the new veterinarian. Then where would you be?"

As soon as the words escaped, she heartily wished she had kept her big mouth shut. Again. What could possibly have possessed her to say such a thing? Ridge lifted an eyebrow and gave her a long, searching look, and she had to hope the heat she could feel in her cheeks wasn't as bright red as it felt.

"I would be happy for you as long as he's a good man who treats you well," Ridge said quietly. For some unaccountable reason, her heart ached sharply. Before she could come up with a response, Destry clambered down the loft ladder. "They're here! I just saw a couple of cars driving up."

The heat in her cheeks spread down her neck and over her shoulders. "Great," she managed to say, trying for a cheerful voice.

"Do you think they'll have Luke with them?"

"I guess we'll find out."

The three of them walked out of the barn into the cold, overcast afternoon just as one SUV pulled up, followed closely by another one. Neither vehicle took the fork in the driveway that led to the foreman's house. They headed toward the main house, pulling into the circular driveway.

Ben climbed out as she, Ridge and Destry approached the vehicles. Her stomach did that ridiculous little jumpy thing again. She had forgotten in the past few hours just how gorgeous the man was. The memory she had been trying without success to forget flooded back into her head in excruciating detail—of walking into the clinic that morning and finding him wet and hard-muscled as he came out of the shower.

She thought of what she had said to her brother. *Maybe I'll just run off with the new veterinarian, and then where would you be?*

The bigger question was, where would *she* be? She could easily see herself making a fool over this man and she had to do her very best to make sure that didn't happen, especially when she couldn't logically find a

way to avoid him, when she trained dogs for a living
and he was the town's only veterinarian.

He waved at them all and held a hand out to Ridge.
"Hi. You must be Caidy's brother."

"Right. I'm Ridge Bowman. This is my daughter,
Destry. I guess you know our Caidy. Nice to meet you.
Welcome to the River Bow."

"Thank you."

The two of them shook hands and then, much to the
girl's astonished delight, Ben shook hands with Destry
too. She grinned at him, braids flying under her cowboy
hat as she turned the handshake into a vigorous exercise.

Ben gave Caidy a friendly sort of smile—much
warmer than any he'd given her so far. Her cheeks
flamed and she didn't miss Ridge's careful look at the
two of them. Drat her big mouth. She should never
have said what she did earlier in the barn. Knowing
her brother, now he was never going to let her forget it.

"I really appreciate you opening the house for us
like this."

Ridge shrugged. "Why not? It's empty. With apologies to my sister-in-law, children ought to be in a house
at Christmastime if they can."

"A little breathing room will certainly make the holidays more comfortable for all of us," he answered. "I've
got someone else back here who's anxious to be on the
River Bow."

He headed to the back of the SUV and reached to
open the hatch.

"You really think Luke is ready to be home?" she
asked.

"He should be. He was moving on his own and
seemed far more comfortable this afternoon than earlier. He's a fighter, this one. You'll still have to keep

a sharp eye on him, but there's no reason he can't be home for that. It'll save you a little on the clinic bill."

All of them converged on the rear of the vehicle. Sure enough, Luke was resting in a travel crate. When he saw her, he whimpered and whined. Ben unlatched the door and the dog's nails scrabbled on the plastic floor of the crate as he tried to stand.

"Easy," Ben said, and his calm voice did the trick. Luke subsided again.

"Hey, Lukey. Hey, buddy." Destry rubbed her cheek against the dog's and scratched under his ears. "You poor thing. Look at that big bandage."

"Hi, Destry. I'm sorry your dog got hurt."

Destry smiled into the backseat, where both Ava and Jack were watching the proceedings with interest.

"Me too. But he's not really my dog. He's one of my aunt Caidy's. I like cats most of all."

"I like cats too," Ava said.

"Not me," Jack answered cheerfully. "I like dogs. This is our dog. His name is Tri."

The dog yipped in answer to his name and Caidy had to smile at the adorable little thing, some kind of chihuahua.

"Can he walk?" Ridge was asking as he studied the injured dog in the crate.

Ben nodded. "He can, but it won't be comfortable for him for a while now. Probably better if we let him take it easy. Do you mind helping me carry him inside?"

"No problem," Ridge said. The two of them carried the crate with Luke inside. Caidy wondered if she should stay with the children or take them inside. Before she could make a decision, Mrs. Michaels joined them from the other vehicle. "You probably want to go help settle your dog, don't you?"

"Yes," she said quickly. "Why don't you all come inside?"

"I think we'll be better off staying put. I'm sure Dr. Caldwell won't be long and the children are anxious to start settling into the house."

She followed the low murmur of men's voices and found them in the kitchen, setting the crate down in the small area she had arranged earlier, in hopes for this very moment.

"Caidy likes to keep her patients right here in the kitchen," Ridge was saying. "This way her bedroom, right down the hall, is close enough to keep an eye on them."

"It's close to the back door for easy trips outside. That's the important thing," she said.

"This works. I like the enclosure," he said. Years ago, she had purchased a small baby play yard that worked well when she was treating an animal whose physical activity needed to be limited.

"Come on out," Ben coaxed the dog. Luke didn't seem to want to move but with their encouragement and Dr. Caldwell helping him along, he rose slowly and hobbled out of the crate, then headed immediately for the soft bed of old blankets she had fashioned in the enclosure.

"What sort of special instructions do I need?"

"Our biggest fear right now is infection. We need to keep the injuries as clean as possible, especially that puncture wound from the bull."

"You don't have to worry about anything," Ridge said. "Caidy's an expert. She used to work at the clinic with Dr. Harris."

"So I hear."

"She should have become a veterinarian," Ridge went on. "It's all she ever wanted to do."

Apparently blabbermouth syndrome ran in the family.

"Is that right?" Ben said, giving her a curious look. She could tell he was wondering why she hadn't pursued her dreams. What was so wrong about a person's life changing direction?

"Yes. I also wanted to be a ballerina when I was eight. And a famous movie star when I was eleven."

And a singer. She decided not to mention she had once wanted to sing professionally. That was another dream she had pushed aside.

"I suppose you're anxious to move into the house. The key is inside on the kitchen table. All the information, like the phone number to the house and the address, are on a paper I've also left for you there."

"Thanks."

One thing she had never anticipated doing with her life was being a landlord to an entirely too sexy veterinarian. Yet here she was. "Call if you have any problems or can't figure out any of the appliances."

"I'm sure we'll be fine. Make sure you let me know if you have any problems with Luke. Here. Let me leave my cell number."

He pulled a business card out of the inside pocket of his coat and left it on the kitchen counter. "If he starts to run a fever or has any other unusual symptoms that concern you, I want you to call me. Day or night."

She doubted she ever would. Even after all her years of working with Doc Harris, she hadn't felt comfortable calling the old veterinarian in the middle of the night.

"Thank you," she answered.

"I'd better head out. The kids are anxious to start decorating their tree."

"Oh. That reminds me. Destry and I dug through our old Christmas things earlier and found a few things we're not using. You're welcome to them."

She picked up the box off the kitchen table and handed it to him. He looked a little disconcerted but then smiled.

"Thank you. I'm sure Mrs. Michaels and the children will find great use for them."

"Not you?"

"I'm sure I'll be roped into helping, like it or not." He looked more resigned than truly reluctant.

"If you'd like, I can carry it out for you while you two get the crate."

"That would be great. Thanks." He smiled at her and she felt those ridiculous flutters again.

"He seems nice," Ridge said after they had loaded the crate and the ornaments and stood on the porch watching the two SUVs head back down the driveway toward the foreman's house.

She thought of how abrupt and harsh he had been the evening before at the clinic. *Nice* wouldn't have been the word she used to describe Ben Caldwell then, but now she was beginning to wonder.

"I guess," she answered in what she hoped was a noncommittal voice.

Ridge gave her a sidelong look. "You might want to think about showing a little more enthusiasm if you plan to run off with the man. At least to him. Occasionally a guy needs a little encouragement."

She rolled her eyes but quickly hurried into the house before Ridge could notice the blush she felt heating her cheeks. She suddenly had a very strong feeling she would have to work hard at being casual and uninterested in order to keep Ridge—and probably the rest of the Bowmans—from trying to do a little matchmaking for Christmas.

A woman's body was a mysterious thing, full of secret hollows and soft, delectable curves.

He was in heaven, warm, sweetly scented heaven. Ben trailed his fingers over the woman in his arms, his hands exploring all those hidden delights. He wanted to stay here forever with his face buried in skin that smelled sweetly of vanilla and rain-washed wildflowers and his hands finding new and exciting terrain to discover.

His body was rock-hard and he pressed against her heat, tangling his fingers in acres of dark, silky hair. She smiled at him out of that sinfully delicious mouth that sent his imagination into overdrive, and her green eyes were bright as springtime. He groaned, his hunger at fever pitch, and kissed her.

Her mouth was as warm and welcoming as the rest of her and when she danced her tongue along his, he groaned and gripped her hands, kissing her with all the pent-up need aching inside him.

"Yes. Kiss me," she murmured in that lilting, musical voice. "Just like that, Ben. Don't stop. Please, don't stop."

All he could think about was burying himself inside. He shifted and prepared to do just that, his body taut and ready, when a phone trilled close to his ear.

He froze…and woke up from the first sexy dream he'd had in ages.

He could still see Caidy Bowman, tangled around him, her body soft and warm, but when he blinked she disappeared.

The phone trilled again and a quick glance at the alarm read 3:00 a.m. Nobody called at this hour unless it was an emergency. He grabbed for it, ignoring the lingering arousal of his body that had no chance in hell of being satisfied by an actual female right now.

"Hello?" he growled.

"I shouldn't have called. I'm sorry." Hearing Caidy Bowman's voice in his ear after he had just heard her in his dreams, pleading with him for more, was so disorienting that for a moment he couldn't process the shift.

"Hello? Are you there?" she asked. The urgency and, yes, fright in her voice pushed away the last clinging tendrils of his sultry dream.

"I'm here. Sorry." He swung his legs over the side of the bed and reached for the jeans he'd left there the night before. "What's wrong? Luke?"

"Yes. He's not… Something's wrong. I wouldn't have called you, except…I don't think it's good. He's struggling to breathe. I thought it might be an infection, but I haven't seen any signs of a fever or anything. I lifted both dressings and they looked clean."

He growled and flipped on the bedside light, then scrubbed at his face to rub the last tendrils of that blasted dream away.

"Give me five minutes."

"Is there something I can do so you don't have to come up here?"

"Probably not. Five minutes."

As he threw on a T-shirt and his jacket, a hundred possibilities raced through his head, very few of them leading to a good outcome. He quickly scribbled a note for Mrs. Michaels and stuck it on her door, though by now she was used to him dashing out in the middle of the night.

Snow lightly gleamed in his headlights as he drove up to the ranch house. He saw lights in the kitchen and pulled as close as he could to the side door on the circular driveway, then hurried up the snow-covered walkway, his emergency kit in his hand.

He didn't even have to rap softly on the door before she yanked it open, her hair tangled around her face and her eyes huge with worry.

"Thank you for coming so quickly. I didn't want to call you but I didn't know what else to do."

He had a strong feeling that wasn't an easy admission for her to make. She struck him as a woman who didn't like relying on others.

Yes. Kiss me. Just like that, Ben. Don't stop. Please, don't stop.

He pushed away the memory of that completely inappropriate dream and did his best not to notice her faded T-shirt or the yoga pants she wore that stretched over every curve, to focus instead on the issue at hand.

"It's fine. I'm here now. Let's see what we have going on."

The dog was clearly in distress, his respiratory rate fast and his breathing labored. His gums and lips were blue and Ben quickly pulled out his emergency oxygen mask and fit it over the dog's mouth and nose.

"It's gotten worse, just in the few minutes since I called you. I don't know what to do."

He ran his hand over the dog's chest and knew instantly what the problem was. He could hear the rattle of air inside the chest cavity with each ragged breath. He bit out an oath.

"What is it?"

"Traumatic pneumothorax. He has air trapped in his chest cavity. We're going to have to get it out. I have a couple of options here. I can take him into the clinic and do an X-ray first, or I can go with my instincts. I can feel the problem. I can try to extract the air with a needle and syringe, which will help his breathing. It's your choice."

She paused for just a moment, then nodded. "I trust you. If you think you can do it here, go ahead."

Her faith in him was humbling, especially given the cold way he had treated her the day before. He fished in his bag for the supplies he would need, then knelt down beside the dog again.

"What can I do?" she asked.

"Try to calm him as best you can and keep him still."

The next few moments were a blur. He was aware of her speaking softly, of her strong, capable hands at his side as she held the dog as firmly as possible. For the most part, he entered that peculiar zone he found whenever he was in the middle of a complicated procedure. He listened with his stethoscope until he could isolate the pneumothorax. The rest was quick and efficient: cleaning the area, inserting the needle in just the right spot, extracting the air with a gurgle, then listening again with the stethoscope to the dog's breath sounds.

This was one of those treatments that was almost instantly effective. Miraculous, even. One moment the dog was frantically struggling to breathe, the next his airway was free and clear and his respiratory rate slowed, his wild trembling with it.

In just moments, he was moving air just as he should through his lungs and had calmed considerably. Satisfied, Ben took the emergency oxygen mask off Luke and returned the syringe to its packaging to be discarded back at the clinic.

"That's it?" Caidy's eyes looked stunned.

"Should be. We're still going to want to watch him closely. If you'd like, I can take him back for another night at the clinic just to be safe."

"No. I… That was *amazing!*"

She was gazing at him as if he had just hung the moon and stars and Jupiter too. He had a funny little ache in his chest, and another inappropriate bit of that crazy dream flashed through his head.

"Thank you. Thank you so much. I was worried sick."

"I'm glad I was close enough to help."

"I'm sorry I had to wake you, though."

So was he. Or he told himself he was anyway. If she hadn't, he probably would have a great deal more of his unruly subconscious to be embarrassed about. "No problem. It was worth it."

"Is there anything else I need to be concerned about?"

"I don't think so. We cleared his lungs. If he has any more breathing trouble, we're going to want to x-ray to see if something else is going on. If you don't mind, I'd like to stick around a little longer to make sure he remains stable."

"Can I get you something? Coffee probably isn't a good idea at three-thirty in the morning if you want to catch a few hours of sleep when we're done here, but we have tea or hot cocoa."

"Cocoa would be good."

He didn't want to think about how comfortable, almost intimate, it was to sit here in this quiet kitchen while the snow fluttered softly against the window and the big log house creaked and settled around them. Only a few moments later, she returned with a couple of mugs of hot chocolate.

"It's from a mix. I thought that would be faster."

"Mix is fine," he answered. "It's all I'm used to anyway."

He took a sip and almost sighed with delight at the rich mix of chocolate and raspberry. "That's not any old mix."

She smiled. "No. I buy from a gourmet food store in Jackson Hole. It's imported from France."

He sipped again, letting the sensuous flavors mix on his tongue. Worth an interrupted night's sleep, just for a little of that divine hot chocolate.

She sat across the table from him and he couldn't help noticing how the loose neckline of her shirt gaped a little with each breath.

"So how is the house working out?"

"Fine, so far. But then, I haven't even had one full night's sleep in it." And what little sleep he *had* enjoyed had been tormented by futile dreams of something he couldn't have.

"I'm sorry again about that, especially considering you had to stay the night with Luke last night."

He shrugged. "Don't be sorry. I didn't mean that. It's just part of my life, something I'm very used to. I often get emergency calls."

Even without the work-related sleep disruptions, his sleep was frequently restless. "The house works well. The kids are happy to have a little more room and Mrs. Michaels is over the moon to have a kitchen again. She made her famous macaroni and cheese for dinner. You'll have to try it sometime. It's as much a gourmet treat as your hot chocolate. I have to admit, I've missed her cooking."

"You must feel very lucky that she was willing to come with you from California."

"Lucky doesn't begin to describe the half of it. I would be completely lost without her. Since Brooke—my wife—died, Anne has kept us all going."

"Of all the places you could have bought a practice, why did you pick Pine Gulch?" She seemed genuinely interested and he leaned back in his chair, sipping at his drink, enjoying the quiet conversation more than he probably should.

"Doc Harris and I have known each other since before I graduated from veterinary school. We met at a conference and had kept up an email correspondence. When he told me he was retiring and wanted to sell his practice, it seemed the perfect opportunity. I had...reasons for wanting to leave California."

She didn't press him, though he could see the curiosity in her eyes. He wanted to tell her. He wasn't sure why—perhaps the quiet peace of the kitchen or the way she had looked at him with such admiration after the thoracentesis. Or maybe just because he hadn't talked about it with anyone, not even Mrs. Michaels.

"My wife has been gone for two years now and I think the kids and I both needed a new start, you know? Away from all the old patterns and relationships. The familiar can sometimes carry its own burdens."

"I can understand that. I've had plenty of moments when I just want to pick up and start over."

What would she want to run from? he wondered. He had a feeling there was far more beneath the surface of Caidy Bowman than a beautiful cowgirl who loved animals and her family.

"So you just packed everybody up and headed to the mountains of Idaho?"

"Something like that."

She sipped at her hot cocoa and they lapsed into silence broken only by the dog's breathing, comfortable and easy now, he was gratified to see. She had a little dab of chocolate on her upper lip and he wondered what she would do if he reached across the table and licked it off.

"Is it rude and intrusive for me to ask about your wife?"

That was one way to squelch his inappropriate desire. He shifted in a chair that suddenly felt as hard and unforgiving as a cold block of cement.

"She…died in a car accident after slipping into a diabetes-related coma while she was behind the wheel."

He didn't add the rest, about the unborn child he hadn't wanted who had died along with her, about how angry he had been with her for the weeks leading up to her death, furious that she would put him in such an untenable position after they had both decided to stop once Jack was born, when doctors warned of the grave risks of a third pregnancy.

He hated himself for the way he had reacted. The temper he had inherited from his grandfather, the one he worked constantly to overcome, had slipped its leash and he had been hateful and mean and had even taken to sleeping in the guest room after she told him she was pregnant, just days after they had decided he would have a vasectomy.

Caidy gave him a sympathetic look, which he definitely did not deserve. "Diabetes. How tragic. She must have been young."

"Thirty."

Her mouth twisted. "I'm sorry. Really sorry."

Yes. Tragic. Something that never should have happened. He blamed himself—and so did Brooke's parents, which was the reason they were trying to poison Ava and Jack against him.

"You must miss her terribly. I can understand why you wanted to make a new start away from the memories."

He did miss her. He had adored her when they first married, until the rather willful, spoiled part of her he had overlooked as part of her charm when they were dating began to show itself in difficult ways.

Brooke had selfishly believed she was stronger than her diabetes. She didn't deserve to have it, thus she shouldn't have to worry about taking care of herself. She was cavalier to the point of recklessness about checking her levels and taking her insulin.

She had been a loving mother, he would never say otherwise, even if he sometimes wondered how a loving mother could risk her own health when she already had so much simply because she wanted more.

"What about you?" he asked to change the subject. "Ever been married?"

She was in midsip with her hot cocoa and coughed a little. "Me? No. I date here and there but…nothing serious. The dating pool around Pine Gulch is a little shallow. I've known most of the unmarried men around here my whole life."

You haven't known me.

The dangerous thought whispered through his mind and seemed to move right in. No. He definitely didn't want to go there. She was a beautiful woman and he was very attracted to her—he only needed to remember that dream if he needed proof—but he would never do anything about that attraction but sneak those tantalizing glimpses at her and wonder.

He had his children to consider and a new practice

he was trying to build. He could see no room for a complicated woman like Caidy Bowman in that picture anywhere.

Why did she hide herself away here in a small town like Pine Gulch? Why hadn't she become a veterinarian? He had the same strange thought of earlier in the day when he had seen her standing on the River Bow porch with her brother and her niece. She was lonely. He had no idea why he thought so, but he was suddenly certain of it.

"So why not dip your feet in other waters? It's a big world. You could always try internet dating."

"Wow. You're a veterinarian *and* a relationship coach. Who would have guessed? It seems an odd combination, but, okay."

He laughed gruffly, only because that was absolutely *not* his usual modus operandi. Usually he was completely oblivious to the interpersonal dramas and entanglements of other people, except when it came to their relationships with their pets.

"That's me. I'll fix up your dog and your broken heart, all for one low fee. And I offer monthly installment plans."

She smiled, the right side of her mouth just a bit higher than the left to create a sweetly pleasing imbalance. The quiet, companionable silence wrapped around them like the trailing tendrils of a woolen scarf.

He wanted to kiss her.

The hunger for a taste—just one little sampling—of chocolate and raspberry and soft, warm woman was intense and bewitching. He needed to get out of there. Now, before he did something completely insane like try to turn his midnight fantasies into reality and received a well-earned slap for it.

The dog snuffled softly and that was the excuse he needed to leave her side and return to the cozy little warren she had created for Luke.

Unfortunately, she followed right behind as he crouched down to check the dog's breathing with his stethoscope.

"How does he sound?"

"Good. Breathing is normal now. I think we solved the problem."

"Thank you again, for everything. I'm not sure Doc Harris could have done the job as well."

Her words seeped inside him. He was inordinately pleased by the compliment. "You're very welcome."

"I hope I don't need to call you in the middle of the night again."

"Please don't hesitate. I'm just down the lane now."

She smiled. "Ridge said it would be like having our own veterinarian-in-residence. Just to put your mind at ease, I promise not to take advantage."

Please. Take advantage all you want. He cleared his throat. "For what it's worth, I think the guys around here are crazy. Even if you did grow up with them."

He wasn't quite sure why he said the words. He was no more a player than he was a relationship coach, for heaven's sake. She flashed him a startled look, her eyes wide and her mouth slightly parted.

He might have left things at that, safe and uncomplicated, except her eyes suddenly shifted to his mouth and he didn't miss the flare of heat in her gaze.

He swore under his breath, already regretting what he seemed to have no power to resist, and then he reached for her.

Chapter Six

As his mouth settled over hers, warm and firm and tasting of cocoa, Caidy couldn't quite believe this was happening.

She was being kissed by the sexy new veterinarian just a day after thinking him rude and abrasive. For a long moment, she was shocked into immobility, then heat began to seep through her frozen stupor. Oh. Oh, yes!

How long had it been since she had enjoyed a kiss and wanted more? She was astounded to realize she couldn't remember. As his lips played over hers, she shifted her neck slightly for a better angle.

She splayed her fingers against his chest—that strong, muscled chest she had seen firsthand just that morning—and his heat soaked into her skin, even through the cotton of his shirt.

Her insides seemed to give a collective shiver. Mmm.

This was exactly what two people ought to be doing at 3:00 a.m. on a snowy December day.

He made a low sound in his throat that danced down her spine and she felt the hard strength of his arms slide around her, pulling her closer. In this moment, nothing else seemed to matter but Ben Caldwell and the wondrous sensations fluttering through her.

This was crazy. Some tiny voice of self-preservation seemed to whisper through her. What was she doing? She had no business kissing someone she barely knew and wasn't even sure if she liked yet. If she kept this up, he was going to think she kissed every guy who happened to smile at her.

Though it took every last ounce of strength, she managed to slide away from all that delicious heat and moved a few inches away from him, trying desperately to catch her breath.

The distance she created between them seemed to drag Ben back to his senses. He stared at her, his eyes as dazed as she felt. "That was wrong. I don't know what I was thinking. Your dog is a patient and…I shouldn't have.…"

She might have been offended by the dismay in his voice if not for the arousal in his eyes and the way he couldn't seem to catch his breath. Because she was having the same sort of reaction—dismay mixed with lingering arousal and a sudden deep yearning—she couldn't very well complain.

His hair was a little rumpled and he had the evening shadow of a beard and all she could think was *yum*.

She cleared her throat, compelled to say something in the strained moment. "Relax, Dr. Caldwell. You didn't do anything wrong, as far as I can see. I didn't exactly push you out the door, did I?"

He ran a hand through his hair. "No. No, I guess you didn't."

"It's late and we're both tired and not quite thinking straight. I'm sure that's all this was."

A muscle flexed in his jaw. He looked as if he would like to argue with her, but after a moment he only nodded. "I'm sure you're right."

"No harm done. We'll both just forget the past five minutes ever happened and go back to our regularly scheduled lives."

"Great idea."

His ready agreement sent a hard kernel of regret to lodge somewhere in her sternum. For a moment, she had felt almost normal, just like any other woman. Someone who could flirt and smile and attract the interest of a sexy male.

He wanted to forget it ever happened, whereas she was quite certain she would never be able to erase these few moments from her memory.

"I should, uh, go."

"Yes." *Or you could stay and kiss me for a few more hours.*

"Call me if anything changes with the dog."

She drew in a breath. "I hope we're past the worst of it. But I will."

That last was a lie. She had absolutely no intention of calling him again in the middle of the night. She would drive Luke to the vet in Idaho Falls before she would drag Ben Caldwell out here again anytime soon.

"Good night."

She nodded, not trusting herself to reply, just wishing he would go already. He gave her a long, searching look before he shrugged back into his ranch coat and left through the side door.

A blast of cold air curled into the room from that brief moment he had opened the door. Chilled by more than just the winter night, she shivered as it sidled under her T-shirt.

What in heaven's name just happened here?

She wrapped her arms around herself. She had *known* he would be trouble. Somehow she had known. She never should have suggested he move into the foreman's house. If she had only used her brain, she might have predicted she would do something stupid around him, like develop a very awkward and embarrassing crush.

She spent most of her days here on the ranch, surrounded by her brothers and his few ranchhands, most of whom were either fresh-faced kids just out of high school or grizzled veterans who either were already married or held absolutely no appeal to her.

The ranch was safe. It had always been her haven from the hardness of the world. Now she had messed that up by inviting a tempting man to set up temporary residence smack in the middle of her comfort zone.

The man certainly knew how to kiss. She couldn't deny that. She pressed a hand to her stomach, which still seemed to be jumping with nerves. The last time she had been kissed so thoroughly and deliciously had been…well, never.

She sighed. It wouldn't happen again. Neither of them wanted this. She had only to remember the stunned dismay in Ben's eyes in that moment when he had come to his senses. He was likely still grieving for his wife, taken from him far too soon. And she…well, she had told herself she wasn't interested in a relationship, that she was content here helping Ridge with Destry and training her dogs and the occasional horse.

For the first time in a long time, she was beginning to wonder what else might be out in the big, scary world, waiting for her.

"I think he's feeling better, don't you?"

Caidy glanced up from the dough she was kneading to see her niece sitting cross-legged beside Luke's blanket. The dog's head was in her lap and he was gazing up at the girl with adoration.

"Yes. I think so. He seems much happier than he was even a few hours ago."

"I'm glad. I really thought he was a goner when I saw old Festus go after him."

Guilt socked her in the gut again. If she had kept a closer eye on Luke, he wouldn't be lying there with those bandages and she wouldn't be so beholden to Ben Caldwell.

"I hope that's a good reminder to you about how dangerous the bulls can be. That could just as easily have been you. I don't ever want you to take a chance with Festus or any of the bulls. They're usually placid guys most of the time, even Festus, but you never know."

"I know. I know. You and Dad have told me that like a thousand times. I'm not a little kid anymore, Aunt Caidy. I'm smart enough to know to keep my distance."

"Good. The ranch can be a dangerous place. You can't ever let your guard down. Even one of the cows could trample you if you lost your footing."

"It's a miracle I ever survived to be eleven years old, isn't it?"

Caidy made a face. "Smarty. You can't blame your dad and me for worrying about you. We just want you to be safe."

And happy, she added silently. She wanted to think

her presence here at the ranch had contributed in that department. If Ridge had been left on his own after Melinda left, forced to employ a string of nannies and babysitters, she wasn't sure Destry would have come through childhood with the same cheerful personality.

"What's going to happen to Luke? You can't train him to be a real cow dog now, can you?"

Even without his injuries, she suspected Luke would always be nervous around the cattle. How could she blame him, especially when she could relate, in a sense? Not to fearing cattle. She had no problem with the big animals. Her fears were a little closer to home. This time of year, her heartbeat always kicked up a bit when the doorbell rang, even when they were expecting company.

The memory of that fateful night was as much a part of her as the sprinkle of freckles on her nose and the tiny scar she had at the outside edge of her left eyebrow from an unfortunate encounter with the business end of a pitchfork when she was eight.

"I'm not really sure yet about Luke," she finally answered Destry as she formed a small ball of dough and set it into the prepared pan. "I'm guessing from this point on, he'll just be a pet."

"Here at the River Bow?"

"Sure. Why not?" They had plenty of dogs and didn't really need another one that was just a pet. Sadie, too old to work, sort of filled that role, but she supposed they would make room for one more.

"Good," Destry said, cuddling the dog close. "It's not his fault he got hurt. Not really. He was only being curious. It doesn't seem fair to get rid of him for an accident."

Destry was a sweet girl, compassionate and loving. Maybe too compassionate sometimes. Caidy smiled, remembering the previous Christmas when she had claimed she didn't want any presents that year. Instead she only wanted cash.

They all learned later she and some of her school-mates were being scammed out of money and belongings…by none other than Gabi, the youngest sister of Trace's new wife.

She hadn't been part of their family then, of course. She had only been a troubled, lost young girl abandoned by her heartless witch of a mother and trying to find her way.

Trace had given both Becca and Gabi the loving family they all deserved—and Gabi and Destry had moved on and become best friends. That wasn't always a good thing. Trouble seemed to find the two of them like a pack of bloodhounds on the scent.

With the dog sleeping soundly now, Destry carefully set his head back down on the blankets, then rose and wandered over to the work island. "Need help rolling out the dough?"

"Sure. I'm doing cloverleaf rolls for dinner this afternoon. You remember, you roll three small balls and stick them together. Wash your hands first."

Destry complied quickly and the two of them worked together in mostly silence for a few moments. Caidy savored these small moments with her niece, who was growing up far too quickly.

She loved making dinner for her family on Sundays, when everyone gathered together to laugh and talk and catch up. Having all these new children—Alex, Maya, Gabi—only made family time together more fun.

She would never be a gourmet chef, but she enjoyed creating meals her family enjoyed. Warm rolls slathered in her homemade jam were her specialty. She still used the recipe her mother had taught her in this very kitchen when she was about Destry's age.

Her life was pretty darn good, she thought as she worked the elastic dough in a kitchen that was warm and comfortable and already smelled delicious from the roast beef that was cooking. She had family and friends, a couple of jobs she enjoyed, a home she loved, a dog who was on the mend.

She didn't need Ben Caldwell blowing into her world, bringing that sweet, rare smile and those stunning kisses, making her feel as if something vital was missing.

"Can I turn on the radio?" Destry asked after a few more minutes.

"Sure. Something we can dance to," she said, pushing away thoughts of Ben with a smile. A moment later, the kitchen filled with music—upbeat Christmas songs. Not really what she had in mind, but what could she do?

Destry was singing "Winter Wonderland" at the top of her lungs and jigging from side to side when the door opened and Ridge came in, stomping snow off his boots.

"It's coming down pretty hard out there. You might be in for a chilly sleigh ride, kiddo."

Destry grinned. "Snow is perfect. What could be more fun? Aunt Caidy already said she would make some of her good hot cocoa and we're going to mix up dough for oatmeal raisin cookies so we can put them in the oven right before we go. That way they'll still be hot on the wagon."

"Sounds like you've got it all figured out."

"It's going to be *great!* Thanks so much for agreeing to take us. You're awesome, Dad."

"You're welcome, kid."

He smiled at his daughter for a moment then turned

to Caidy. She noticed with no small degree of apprehension the deceptively casual expression on her brother's rugged features. "Hey, how would you feel if we added a few more at dinner?"

It wasn't a completely unusual request. Ridge had a habit of inviting in strays. She took care of the four-legged kind, and he often focused on the human variety.

"Shouldn't be a problem. It's a big roast and I can always throw in a few more potatoes and add more carrots. Who did you invite?"

He shrugged. "Just the new vet and his kids."

Just the new vet? The man she happened to have tangled lips with in this very kitchen twelve hours earlier? The very man she was trying to shove out of her brain. She opened her mouth to answer but nothing came out except an embarrassing sort of squeak.

"He was out shoveling when I cleared the drive with the tractor and we started chatting. I mentioned dinner and then the sleigh ride after and asked if they would like to join us."

She suddenly wanted to take the ball of dough in her hand and fling it at her brother. How could he do this to her? She had warned him not to get any ideas in his head about matchmaking, yet here he was doing exactly that.

She supposed she shouldn't be so surprised. All three of her brothers seemed to think their mission in life was to set her up with some big, gorgeous cowboy. Ben wasn't exactly a cowboy, but he had the big and gorgeous parts down.

How was she supposed to sit across the dinner table from the man when all she could remember was the silky slide of his tongue against hers, the hardness of those muscles against her, his sexy, ragged breathing as he tasted her mouth?

"You don't mind, do you?"

She would have laughed if she suddenly wasn't feeling queasy.

"No. Why should I mind?" she muttered, while in her head she went through about a dozen reasons. Starting and ending with that kiss.

"That's what I figured. You and Becca and Laura are always making way too much food. Inviting the vet and his family for dinner seemed like a nice way to welcome them to the ranch. And I figured his kids might get a charge out of going with us on the sleigh ride later."

Of all her three brothers, Ridge was the most taciturn. His failed marriage and the burden of responsibility that came with running the family ranch while the twins pursued other interests made him seem hard sometimes, but he also showed these flashes of kindness that tugged at her heart.

"I'm sure they will. It's bound to be something new and exciting for a couple of kids from California. They probably don't have much snow where they're from."

"Awesome!" Destry exclaimed. "I hope they're good singers."

Right. Singing and Ben Caldwell. Two things she should avoid at all costs thrown right in her face. This should prove to be a very interesting evening.

Chapter Seven

"Do you think Alex and Maya will be there?"

"It's a good bet, kid," Ben told his son as the three of them walked down the plowed lane through the gentle snowfall toward the ranch house. The snow muted all sounds, even the low gurgle of the creek, on the other side of the trees that formed an oxbow around the ranch.

The cold air smelled of hay and pine and woodsmoke. He breathed deeply, thinking it had been far too long since he had taken time to just savor his surroundings. The River Bow was unexpectedly serene, with the mix of aspens and pine and the mountains soaring to the east.

"I hope Gabi is there," Ava said, looking more enthusiastic about the outing than she had about anything in a long time. "She's superfunny."

"I'm sure she will be. Ridge said their whole family was coming for dinner and she's part of the family."

He and his kids, however, were *not*. They were only temporary guests and he probably had no business dragging his children to their family dinner, especially after the events of the night before.

He should have said no. Ridge Bowman took him by surprise with the invitation while they were out clearing snow and he had been so caught off guard, he hadn't known quite how to reply.

The kids would enjoy it. He had known that from the get-go. He was fairly sure he wouldn't. He didn't mind socializing. Brooke had loved to throw parties and some part of him had missed that since her death. But this party was obviously a family thing and he hated to impose.

If that wasn't enough, he also wasn't ready to face a certain woman yet—Caidy Bowman, of the soft curves and the silky hair and the warm mouth that tasted like cocoa and heaven.

That kiss, coming on the heels of his vivid, sexy dream about her, left him aching and restless. He hadn't slept at all after he left her house. He had tossed and turned and punched his pillow until he had finally gotten up at 6:00 a.m., before the children, and started shoveling snow to burn away some of this edgy hunger. Mother Nature had dumped quite a bit of snow throughout the day, so he had plenty of chances to work it off.

That kiss. He had wanted to drown in it, just yank her against him and tease and taste and explore until they were both shaking with need. Somehow he knew she would respond just as he had dreamed, with soft, eager enthusiasm.

How did a guy engage in casual chitchat with a woman after he had kissed her like that without wanting to do it all over again?

Despite the December chill, he unzipped his coat. He probably couldn't do much about his overheated imagination, but the rest of him didn't need to simmer.

A couple of dogs came up to greet them as they approached the house and Jack eased behind him. Though his son saw plenty of strange dogs at the clinic, he was often apprehensive around animals he didn't know. A large, untrained mastiff had cornered him once at the clinic a few years earlier, intent only on friendliness, but Jack had been justifiably frightened by the encounter and wary ever since.

"They won't hurt you, Jack. See, both of their tails are wagging. They just want to say hi."

"I don't want to," Jack said, hiding even further behind him.

"You don't have to, then. Ava, can you carry the bag with Mrs. Michaels's salad and toffee while I give your brother a lift?"

She grabbed the bag away from him and hurried ahead while he scooped up his son and set him on his shoulders for the last hundred yards of the walk, much to Jack's delight. It wouldn't be long before the boy grew too large for this but for now they both enjoyed it, even with his son's snowy boots hitting his chest.

In the gathering dusk, the log ranch house was lit up with icicle lights that dripped from the eaves and around the porch. People on the coast would pay serious money for the chance to spend Christmas here at a picturesque cattle ranch in the oxbow of a world-class fly-fishing creek.

Several unfamiliar vehicles were parked in the circular driveway in front of the ranch house and that awkwardness returned. If not for his children's anticipation, he probably would have turned on his heels and headed back to the cottage.

Ava reached the porch before they did and skipped up the stairs to ring the doorbell. As Ben and Jack reached the steps a woman he didn't know with dark hair and a winsome smile answered. "You must be the new veterinarian. Ridge mentioned you and your family were joining us. Hi. I'm Becca Bowman, married to Trace. Come in out of the snow."

He walked inside and went to work divesting the children of their abundance of outerwear: coats, gloves, hats, scarves and boots. Becca gathered them all up and set them inside a large closet under the curving log staircase.

"Are you Gabi's mom?" Ava asked, sitting on the bottom step to slip out of her boots.

"I'm her big sister actually. It's a long story. But I guess in every way that matters, I'm her mother."

An intriguing story. He wondered at the details but decided they weren't important. Becca had obviously stepped up to raise her sister and he couldn't help but find that admirable.

"Where is Gabi?" Ava asked eagerly.

"She and Destry are around somewhere. They'll be so excited to see you. They've been waiting impatiently for you to get here for the past hour."

Ava beamed with an enthusiasm that had been missing for far too long. Maybe staying here at the ranch near a friend for a few weeks would be good for her. Maybe it would finally help her resign herself to their move to Idaho, to the distance now between her and her grandparents.

"Last I saw them, they were playing a video game in the den. Straight down that hall and to the left."

Ava took off, with Jack close on her heels. He thought about calling them back but decided to let them figure things out. Kids usually did a much better job of that than adults.

"I think dinner is nearly ready," Becca said to him. "Come on into the great room and I'm sure one of the boys can hook you up with something to drink."

She led him into a huge room dominated by a massive angled wall of windows and the big Christmas tree he had seen glimmering from outside as they approached. Where was Caidy? he wondered, then was embarrassed at himself for looking for her straight away.

Her brother Ridge headed over immediately with a cold beer. "Hey, Doc Caldwell. Glad you could make it."

At least one of them was. "Thanks."

"Have you met my brothers?" Ridge asked.

"I know Chief Bowman. Fire Chief Bowman," he corrected. He could only imagine how confusing that must be for the town, to have a fire chief and police chief who were not only brothers but identical twins.

"You've deserted us at the inn, I understand," Taft Bowman said.

He winced. The only thing that bothered him worse than being obligated to Caidy was knowing he had checked out prematurely from the Cold Creek Inn. "Sorry. We were bursting at the seams there."

"Oh, no worries about that. Laura's already booked your rooms through the holiday. She had to turn away several guests in the past few weeks and ended up contacting some of them who wanted to be on standby. They were thrilled at the last-minute cancellation."

He had expected the immensely popular inn would do just fine without his business. "That's a relief."

"She's been saying for a week how she thought your

kids needed to be in a real house for the holidays. She was thrilled when Caidy talked to her about having you stay here. As soon as she hung up the phone, she said she couldn't believe she'd never thought of the foreman's cottage out here."

"I'm already missing those delicious breakfasts at the inn," he said. That was true enough, though Mrs. Michaels was also an excellent cook and had taken great delight just that morning in preparing pancakes from scratch and her famous fluffy scrambled eggs.

In his three weeks of staying at the Cold Creek Inn, Laura Bowman had struck him as an extraordinarily kind woman. The whole family, really, had welcomed him and his children to town with warm generosity.

"The guy over there on his cell phone is my husband, Trace," Becca said. "He's the police chief and is lucky enough to be off duty tonight, though his deputies often forget that."

The man in question waved and smiled a greeting but continued on the phone. Ben suddenly remembered the toffee and pulled out the tin. "Where would you like me to put this?"

"You didn't have to fix anything," Becca scolded.

"I didn't have anything to do with it," he admitted. "My housekeeper did all the heavy lifting. She sends her apologies, by the way. She would have come but she needed to take a call from her daughter. She's expecting her first grandchild and the separation has been difficult."

He felt more than a little guilty about that. Anne had come with them to Idaho willingly enough but he knew she missed her daughter, especially during this exciting, nerve-racking time of impending birth. They communicated via videoconferencing often, but it wasn't the same as face-to-face interaction.

"Let's just set it on the table here. Wow. I've got to taste some first. I love toffee."

"Ooh, send some this way," Taft said, so Becca passed the tin of candy around to all the brothers.

"She also made a salad. Greek pasta."

"That sounds delicious too. I'll take it in to see where Caidy wants it."

"I can do that." His words—and anticipation to see her again—came out of nowhere. "I should probably check in on my patient while I'm here anyway."

"Okay. Sure. Just through the hall and around the corner."

He remembered. He had a feeling every detail of the Bowman kitchen would be etched in his memory for a very long time.

When he entered, his gaze immediately went to Caidy, and the restlessness that had dogged him all day seemed to ease. She stood at the stove with her hair tucked into a loose ponytail, wearing an apron over jeans and a crisp white shirt.

She looked pretty and fresh, and something soft and warm seemed to unfurl inside him.

She must have sensed his presence, though it was obvious she was spinning a dozen different plates. She glanced around and he saw her cheeks turn pink, though he wasn't certain if it was from the heat of the stove or the memory of the kiss they had shared in this very room.

"Oh. Hi. You're here."

"Yes. I've brought a salad. Greek pasta. My house-keeper made it, actually. And toffee. I brought toffee too."

Good grief. Could he sound any more like an idiot?

"That's great. Thank you. The salad can go on the buffet in the dining room. I don't imagine the toffee will last long with my brothers around."

"They were already working on it," he said.

"Oh, man. I love toffee. They know it, too, but do you think they're going to save me any? Highly doubtful. It's going to be gone before I get a taste."

"I'll have Mrs. Michaels make more for you," he offered, his voice gruff.

She smiled. "That's sweet of you. Or I could just arm wrestle my brothers for the last piece."

"Right." He cleared his throat. "Uh, I'll just take this into the dining room."

This was stupid. Why couldn't he talk to her? Yes, she was a beautiful, desirable woman who had moaned in his arms just a few hours earlier, but that didn't mean he couldn't carry on a semi-intelligent conversation with her.

Determined to do just that, after he had taken the salad into the dining room he returned to the kitchen instead of seeking the safety of the great room with the rest of the Bowmans.

Caidy looked surprised to see him again so soon.

"I wanted to check on Luke," he explained.

"He seems to be feeling better. I moved him into my room so he has a chance to rest during all the commotion of dinner."

"You mind if I take a look at him?"

She glanced up, surprise in her eyes. "Really? You don't have to do that. Ridge didn't invite you to dinner to get free vet care out of the deal."

Why *had* Ridge invited him? He had been wondering that all afternoon. "I'm here. I might as well see how he's progressing."

"Can I take over stirring the gravy so you can show Ben to your room?"

For the first time, he noticed Laura Bowman, who had been standing on the other side of the kitchen slicing olives.

"Thank you. It should be done in just a few minutes."

Caidy washed her hands, then tucked a loose strand of hair behind her ear, nibbling her lip between her teeth just enough to remind him of how that lip had tasted between his own teeth and sent blood pooling in his groin.

She led the way down the hall to a door just off the kitchen and he heard a little bark from inside the room just before she pushed open the door.

He had a vague impression of, not so much fussiness, as feminine softness. A lavender-and-brown quilt and a flurry of pillows covered a queen-size bed, and lace curtains spilled from the windows. His gaze was drawn to a lovely oil painting of horses grazing in a flower-strewn field that looked as if it could be somewhere on the River Bow. It hung on the wall at the foot of the bed, the first thing she must see upon awakening and drifting off to sleep.

He shouldn't be so interested in where she slept— or what she might dream about—he ordered himself, and he quickly shifted attention to the dog. The border collie was lying beside the bed near the window, in the same enclosure he had rested in while in the kitchen.

When he saw Caidy, Luke wagged his tail and tried to get up but she bent over and rested a comforting hand on his head. He immediately subsided as if she had tranquilized him.

"Look who's here. It's our friend Dr. Caldwell. Aren't you glad to see him?"

Because he had spent two hours operating on the dog and shoved a needle into his lungs a few hours earlier, Ben highly doubted he ranked very high on the animal's list of favorite humans, but he wasn't going to argue with her.

"No more breathing trouble?"

"No. He slept like a rock the rest of the night and has been sleeping most of the day."

"That's the best thing for him."

"That's what I figured. I've been keeping his pain medication on a consistent schedule. Ridge has been helping me carry him outside for his business."

He stepped over the enclosure and knelt inside so he could run his hand over the dog. Though he focused on his patient, some part of him was aware the whole time of her watching him intently.

Did she feel the tug and pull between them, or was it completely one-sided?

He didn't think so. She had definitely kissed him back. He vividly relived the sweetness of her mouth softening under his, the little catch in her breathing, the way her pulse had raced beneath his fingers. His gut ached at the memory, especially at the knowledge that a memory and those wild dreams were all he was likely to have from her.

"I think he's healing very nicely. I would think in a day or two you can let him have full mobility again. Bring him into the office around the middle of the week and I can check the stitches. I'm happy to see he's doing so well."

"You didn't think he would survive, did you?"

"No," he said honestly. "I'm always happy when I'm proved wrong."

"You've really gone above and beyond in caring for him. Coming out in the middle of the night and everything. I…want you to know I appreciate it. Very much."

He shrugged. "It's my job. I wouldn't be very good at it if I didn't care about my patients, would I?"

She opened her mouth as if to say something else but then closed it again. Awkwardness sagged between them, heavy and clumsy, and he suddenly knew she was remembering the kiss too.

He sighed. "Look, I need to apologize about last night. It was…unprofessional and should never have happened."

She gazed at him out of those impossibly green eyes without blinking and he wondered what the hell she might be thinking.

"I don't want you to think I'm in the habit of that."

"Of what?"

He felt stupid for bringing it up but didn't know how else to move past this morning-after sort of discomfort. Better to face it head-on, he figured. "You know what. I came over to help you with your dog. I shouldn't have kissed you. It was unprofessional and shouldn't have happened."

Unexpectedly, she gave a strained-sounding laugh. "Maybe you ought to think about adding that to your list of services, Dr. Caldwell. Believe me, if word got out what a good kisser you are, every woman in Pine Gulch who even *thought* about owning a cat or dog would be lining up at the adoption day at the animal shelter just for the perk of being able to lock lips with the sexy new veterinarian."

He could feel himself flush. She was making fun of

him, but he supposed he deserved it. "I was only trying to tell you there's no reason to worry it will happen again. It was late and I was tired and not really myself. I never would have even *thought* about kissing you otherwise."

"Oh, well. That explains it perfectly, then."

He had the vague feeling he had hurt her feelings somehow, which absolutely hadn't been his intention. He suddenly remembered how much he had hated the dating scene, trying to wade through all those nuances and layers of meaning.

"Good to know your weaknesses," she went on. "Next time I need veterinary care in the middle of the night for one of my animals, I'll be sure to call the vet over in Idaho Falls. We certainly wouldn't want a repeat of that hideous experience."

"I think we can both agree it wasn't hideous. Far from it." He muttered the last bit under his breath but she caught it anyway. Her pupils flared and her gaze dipped to his mouth again. His abdominal muscles contracted and he felt that awareness seethe and curl between them again, like the currents of Cold Creek.

"Just unfortunate," she murmured.

"Give me a break here, Caidy. What do you want me to say?"

"Nothing. We both agreed to forget it happened."

"That's a little easier said than done," he admitted.

"Isn't everything?"

"True enough."

"It's no big deal, Ben. We kissed. So what? I enjoyed it, and you enjoyed it. We both agree it shouldn't happen again. Let's just move on, okay?"

As easy as that? Somehow he didn't think so, but he wasn't about to argue.

"I should get back to the kitchen. Thank you for taking the time to check on Luke."

"No problem," he said. He followed her out of the room, wishing more than anything that circumstances could be different, that he could be the sort of man a woman like Caidy Bowman needed.

Chapter Eight

Insufferable man!

When they left her bedroom, Ben headed into the great room with the others while Caidy, unsettled and annoyed, returned to the kitchen to finish the preparations for dinner.

How could he reduce what had been one of the single most exhilarating moments of her life to a terrible mistake teeming with awkwardness?

Yes, the kiss shouldn't have happened. They both accepted it. He didn't have to act as if the two of them had committed some horrible crime and should beat themselves up with guilt about it for the rest of their lives.

It was late and I was tired and not really myself. I never would have even thought *about kissing you otherwise.*

That removed any doubt in her mind that he was attracted to her. He had kissed her because he was tired and because she was there. The humiliation of that was almost more than she could bear, especially given the enthusiastic way she had responded to him and the silly fantasies she had been spinning all day.

"Is something wrong? Are you ready for us to start taking dishes out to the dining room?" Becca asked.

With a jolt, Caidy realized she had been staring without moving at the roast she had taken out of the oven. She frowned, frustrated at herself and at Ben, and did her best to drag her attention away from her pout.

"Yes. That would be great, thank you. Everything should be just about ready to go. I ought to let the roast sit for another few minutes, but by the time we get everything else on the table, it will be ready to carve."

Becca and Laura picked up covered bowls and took them out to the table, chattering as they went about their respective plans for Christmas Eve. Caidy smiled as she listened to them. She loved both of her sisters-in-law deeply. Having sisters had turned out to be far more wonderful than she ever imagined. The best part about them was that each was perfect for her respective Bowman brother.

Becca, with that hidden vulnerability and her flashes of clever humor, brought out the very best in Trace. Since she and Gabi had come into his life the previous Christmas, Caidy had seen a soft gentleness in Trace that had been missing since their parents were murdered.

Laura Pendleton was exactly the woman Caidy had always wanted for Taft to soothe the wildness in him. Taft and Laura had once been deeply in love until their engagement abruptly and mysteriously ended just days before their wedding.

Seeing them together, reunited after all these years,

filled her with delight. She especially loved seeing Taft shed his carefree player image and step up to be a caring father to Laura's two children, energetic Alex and the adorable Maya.

She wasn't jealous of the joy her brothers had found—she was happy for them all. Maybe she grew a little wistful when she watched those sweet little moments between two people who loved each other deeply, but she did her best not to think about them.

Still chattering, both Laura and Becca came back into the kitchen to grab the salads they had each prepared out of the refrigerator. At least the Sunday dinners had become much easier since her brothers married. She used to fix the whole shebang on her own, but now the two women and often Gabi pitched in and contributed their own salads or desserts.

She didn't know how much longer this Sunday dinner tradition could continue. She wouldn't blame Taft and Trace for wanting to spend their free time with their own nuclear families. For now, everyone seemed content to continue gathering each week when they could.

"So the new veterinarian is gorgeous. Why didn't anybody tell me?" Becca said, putting the rolls Caidy had removed from the second oven into a basket.

"I don't know," Laura answered. "Maybe we figured since you're married to Trace Bowman, who is only second in all-around gorgeousness to his twin brother, you really didn't need to know about the cute new vet."

Caidy felt another of those little pangs of envy at Becca's sudden cat-who-ate-the-canary smile.

"True," she answered. "But you should have warned me before I opened the door to find this yummy man on the doorstep—and added to the yum factor, the very adorable little boy on his shoulders."

Caidy didn't say anything as she carved the roast beef. This was usually Ridge's job, for some reason, but she didn't want to call him in from entertaining said veterinarian out in the other room.

"What about you, Caidy?" Becca said. "You're the only available one here. Don't you think he's gorgeous? Something about those big blue eyes and those long, long lashes…"

She had a sudden vivid memory of those eyes closing as he kissed her the night before, of his mouth teasing and licking at hers, of the heat and strength of his arms around her and how she had wanted to lean into that broad chest and stay right there.

Her knees suddenly felt a little on the weak side and she narrowly avoided slicing off her thumb.

"Sure," she said. "Too bad he's got the personality of a honey badger."

She didn't miss the surprised looks both women gave her. Laura's mouth opened and Becca's eyebrows just about crept up to her hairline, probably because Caidy rarely spoke poorly about anyone. Every time she started to vent about someone when they weren't present, her mother's injunction about not saying something behind a person's back you wouldn't say to his face would ring in her ears.

She wouldn't have said anything if she wasn't burning with humiliation about that kiss he obviously regretted.

Laura was the first to speak. "That's odd you would say that. I found him very nice while he was staying at the inn. Half of my front desk staff was head over heels in love with him from the start."

After that kiss, she was very much afraid it wouldn't take more than a slight jostle for her to join them. She couldn't remember ever being this drawn to a man—the fact that she was so attracted to a man who basically found her a nuisance was just too humiliating.

"I'm not surprised," she finally said, hoping they would attribute the color she could feel soaking her cheeks to the overwarm kitchen and her exertions fixing the meal. "Do you want to know what I think about Ben Caldwell? I think he's a rude, arrogant, opinionated jerk. Some women are drawn to that kind of man. Don't ask me why."

"Don't forget, he's also often inconveniently in the wrong place at the wrong time."

At the sudden deep voice, she and both of her sisters-in-law gave a collective gasp and turned to the doorway. Every single molecule inside her wanted to cringe at the sight of Ben standing there, watching the three of them, his face void of expression.

"My son spilled a glass of water," he explained. "I came in looking for a towel to clean it up. Unless you think that's too rude of a request."

Becca reached almost blindly into the drawer where Caidy kept the dish towels, pulled one out and handed it to him.

"Thanks," he answered, then left without another word. Caidy wanted to bury her face in the gravy.

"Wow. I guess the two of you haven't exactly hit it off," Becca said.

Caidy thought of that sizzling kiss, apparently mostly one-sided. "You could say that," she answered.

Her mother would have yanked her earlobe and sent her to her bedroom for being so unconscionably rude to a guest in their home. She couldn't face him again. How could she sit at the table beside him after what he had heard her say? The worst of it was, none of it was true. She was just being petty and small, embarrassed that she was so fiercely attracted to a man who regretted ever touching her.

How could she figure out a way to stay here in the kitchen all evening?

She let out a heavy breath. She was going to have to find a way to apologize to him, but how on earth could she manage that without giving him some kind of explanation? She couldn't tell him the truth. That would only add another layer of mortification onto her humiliation.

"Um, I think I'll just take these rolls out," Becca said into the sudden painful silence.

After she hurried out of the kitchen, Laura placed a hand on Caidy's arm. "Okay, what was that about? Did something happen between the two of you?"

Her dear friend had known her for many years— long before her parents were killed, when everything in her world changed. She didn't want to tell her. She didn't want to talk to *anyone*—she just wanted to hide out in her room with Luke. He, at least, was one male she didn't feel awkward and stupid around.

She sighed. "I called him to come over last night. One of those frantic, middle-of-the-night emergencies. Luke was having trouble breathing and I was upset and didn't know what else to do. He… Before he left, he… We kissed. It was…great. Really great. But today he told me what a mistake it was. He acted like it was this horrible experience that we should both pretend never happened. I guess I was more hurt than I realized by his reaction. I lashed out, which wasn't fair. I don't believe any of those things. Well, I did at first. He was quite rude to me after Luke's accident and treated me like it was my fault. I guess it was, in some ways, but he really twisted the knife. He's been… We've been fine since then, except just now in my room."

Laura was silent for a moment, apparently digesting that barrage of information. Finally she spoke with that calm common sense Caidy loved about her.

"I've had the chance over the past few weeks while he's been staying at the inn to talk with Mrs. Michaels," she said. "She's told me a few things about Ben's situation. More than she probably should have, probably. Take it easy on the man, okay? He's been through a rough few years. His wife's death was horrible apparently."

"He told me she died of complications from diabetes."

"Did he also tell you she was pregnant at the time?"

"No. Oh, no."

Laura nodded. "Apparently she went into a diabetic coma while she was driving and crashed into a tree. Their baby died along with her. It was a miracle Ava and Jack weren't in the car too. They were with their grandparents."

Those poor children. And poor Ben. If she felt bad before about what she had said, now she felt about a zillion times worse.

"According to Mrs. Michaels, his late wife's parents blame him for their daughter and grandchild's death and have done all they can to drive Ava and Jack away from him. That's the main reason he came here, I believe. To put some distance between them and try salvaging his family."

She paused and squeezed Caidy's arm. "I think he could really use a friend."

She had never considered herself a petty person before but she was beginning to discover otherwise. So what if the man regretted kissing her? So her pride was bruised. She tried to be a good person most of the time. Couldn't she look past that and be that friend Laura was talking about?

"Thanks for telling me. I'll…figure out a way to apologize. But not right now, okay? Right now I have a dozen people to feed."

Laura hugged her. "I know you will. Apologize, I mean. You're a good person, Caidy. Someone I'm pleased to call my sister. I just have one more question and it's an important one. I want you to think long and hard before you answer me."

She felt more than a little trepidation. "What's that?"

"Besides being arrogant and rude, how is our Dr. Caldwell in the kissing department?"

Despite everything, she gave a strained laugh. "Let me put it this way. Luke wasn't the only one having trouble breathing last night."

Laura grinned at her, which gave her a little burst of courage. Enough, at least, that she could draw in a deep breath, pick up the platter with the roast beef slices and head out into the other room with squared shoulders to face what just might be the most embarrassing meal of her life.

Dinner wasn't quite the ordeal she had feared.

By the time she reached the table, the only seat left was at the opposite end of the table from Ben, between Ridge at the head and Destry. Good. She needed a little space from Ben while she tried to figure out how she could possibly face the man after making a complete idiot of herself over him, again and again.

He was deep in conversation with her brothers and Becca when she sat down, and he didn't look in her direction, much to her relief. After Ridge said grace, blessing the food and welcoming their guests to the ranch, various conversations flowed around her. Caidy moved her food around in silence, for the most part, until Destry, Gabi and Ava enlisted her opinion about how old she was when she started wearing makeup.

She didn't wear much now unless she was dressing up for something. "I think I was about thirteen or fourteen before I wore anything but lip gloss. You've got a few years to go, girls."

"I'm ready now," Gabi declared.

"Me too," Destry chimed in.

"My grandma let me keep some eye makeup and lip stuff at her house when we lived in California," Ava said. "I could only put it on while I was there or when we went shopping or out to lunch. I had to wash it off before I left so my dad didn't freak, which was totally stupid."

Destry looked slightly appalled at the idea of keeping makeup—or anything else—from her father. "I could never do that!"

"My grandma said it was okay."

In the mode of adults sticking together, Caidy gave the three girls a mild look. "Here's a pretty good rule— if you can't wear it, taste it or say it in front of your dad, you probably shouldn't wear it, taste it or say it when he's not there."

"Agreed." Ridge interjected into the conversation. "You hear that, Des?"

The three girls giggled and started talking about something from school, leaving Caidy's mind to follow the conversation between the twins and Ben at the other end of the table.

"So, Dr. Caldwell, how are you finding Pine Gulch?" Trace was asking.

"Ben. Please, call me Ben. We're enjoying living here so far. The town seems to be filled with very kind people. For the most part anyway."

He didn't look in her direction when he spoke but she cringed anyway, certain his pointed barb was aimed at her.

"It's the *least part* you have to worry about," Taft said with a wink. "I could name a few people in town whose bad side you want to stay far clear of. I'm sure Trace knows a few more on the law enforcement side. We've got our share of bad customers."

"I'm sure you do," Ben murmured. "Rude, arrogant jerks."

"You better believe it," Taft said.

Becca quickly cleared her throat. "Uh, can you pass the potatoes?" she asked Ben.

"Sure, if there are any left." He picked up the bowl Caidy always served the mashed potatoes in, the flower-lined earthenware that had always been one of her mother's favorites.

For the first time since she sat down, he looked in her direction, though his gaze was focused somewhere above her head. "Everything is really delicious," he said. "Isn't that right, Ava? Jack?"

"Supergood," Jack said. He had a smudge of gravy on his cheek and looked absolutely adorable. "Can I have another roll? Ooh, with jam! I *love* strawberries."

Ben grabbed one of her cloverleaf rolls and spread some of her jam on it. When he handed it to his son, Jack gobbled it in three bites, smearing red along with the gravy. Ben shook his head, picked up his napkin and dabbed at the mess on Jack's face. She watched out of the corner of her gaze as those big hands that had held her close attended to his child, and something soft and warm unfurled inside her chest.

He looked up at just that moment and caught her watching. Their gazes held for one long, charged moment while the conversation flowed around them. Then Ridge asked him another question and he looked away, breaking the connection.

He and his children fit in well with the family. Taft's stepson, Alex, and Jack seemed like two peas in a proverbial pod, with Maya attending closely to their every word, and Gabi and Des had been quick to absorb Ava into their circle.

This was only temporary, she reminded herself. After the holidays, he would take his cute kids and his friendly housekeeper and move into the big house he was building. In a matter of days, he would be just a peripheral figure in her world. He wouldn't even be that if she didn't need to take one of the dogs for the occasional visit to the veterinarian.

She should be relieved about that, she told herself. Not glum.

"I love that painting over the fireplace," Ben said into a temporary lull of the conversation. "I see the artist's last name is Bowman. Any relation?"

The rest of the table fell silent—even the children. Nobody seemed willing to jump in to answer him except Ridge.

"Yes," her oldest brother finally said. "She is a relation. She was our mother."

Ben glanced around the table, obviously picking up on the sudden shift in mood.

"I'll admit, I don't know much about art, but I find that piece striking. I don't know if it's the horses in the foreground or the mountains or the fluttery curtains in the window of the old cabin but every time I look away for a few moments, something draws me back. That's real talent."

Her heart warmed a little at his praise of their mother's talent. "She was brilliant," Caidy murmured.

He looked at her and she saw an unexpected compassion in his eyes. Seeing it made her feel even more guilty. She didn't deserve compassion from him, not after her mean words.

"Several of her paintings were stolen eleven years ago," Trace said. "Since then, we've done our best to recover what we can. We've had investigators tracking some of them down. This one was located about three years ago in a gallery in the Sonoma area of California."

"It was always Caidy's favorite," Ridge put in. "Finding it again was something of a miracle."

This shifted all attention to her again and she squirmed. Did anybody besides Laura and Becca pick up the tension in the room? She doubted it. Her brothers usually were oblivious to social currents and the kids were too busy eating and talking and having fun. Just as they should be.

To her relief, Laura—sweet, wonderful Laura—stepped up to deflect attention. "So, Dr. Caldwell, you and your children are coming along on the sleigh ride after dinner, aren't you?"

"Sleigh ride!" Jack exclaimed and he and Alex, best buddies now, did a cute little high-five maneuver.

Ben watched them ruefully. "I don't know. I kind of feel like we've intruded enough on your family."

"Oh, you have to come," Destry exclaimed.

"Yes!" Gabi joined her. "It's going to be awesome!

We're going to sing Christmas carols and have hot chocolate and everything. Oh, please, come with us!"

If things weren't so funky between them right now, she would have told him he was fighting a losing battle. One man simply couldn't fight the combined efforts of the Bowmans and their progeny, adopted or otherwise.

"We're not going far," Ridge promised. "Only a couple miles up the canyon. Probably shouldn't take more than an hour."

"Resistance is futile," Taft said with a grin. "You might as well give in gracefully."

Ben laughed. "In that case, sure. Okay."

The kids shrieked with excitement. Caidy wished she could share even a tiny smidgen of their enthusiasm. The only bright spot for her in the whole thing was that Ben's presence probably eliminated the need for her to go along. Ridge couldn't claim they didn't have enough adults now. She would just offer an excuse to stay at the house and let the rest of them have all the Christmas fun.

She was still going to have to figure out a way to apologize to the man, but at this point she would take any reprieve she could find, however temporary.

Chapter Nine

After dinner had been cleared, the girls' other friends began arriving. Caidy threw in the trays of cookies she and Destry had readied, her brothers headed out to hitch up the big draft horses to the hay wagon and everyone else began donning winter gear. After the cookies came out, Caidy walked through the house gathering all the blankets she could find.

As she headed down the stairs with an armload of blankets, she saw through the big windows that the snow had eased and was only falling now in slow, puffy flakes. Moonlight had peeked behind the storm clouds, turning everything a pearlescent midnight-blue.

It was stunning enough from here. She could only imagine how beautiful it would be to ride through the night on the wagon, with the cold air in her face and the sound of children's laughter swirling through the night.

She was almost sorry she wasn't going with them. Almost.

She continued down the stairs, doing her best to avoid making eye contact with Ben, who was helping Jack into his boots.

"Sleigh ride. Sleigh ride. Sleigh ride," Maya chanted, wiggling her hips that were bundled up along with the rest of her in a very cute pink snowsuit with splashy orange flowers.

Caidy couldn't help laughing. "You're going to have a wonderful time, little bug," she said, kissing Maya's nose. She loved all of the children in her family but sweet, vulnerable Maya held a special place in her heart.

"You come," Maya said, reaching for her hand.

"Oh, honey. I'm not going. I'll be here when you get back."

"What do you mean, you're not going? You have to come," Ridge said sternly. "Where's your coat?"

"In the closet. Where it's staying. I figured somebody needs to stay here. Keep the home fire burning and all that."

"Don't worry about that," Becca said from underneath Trace's arm. "I've got that covered."

For the first time, Caidy realized her sister-in-law wasn't wearing a coat either.

"Why aren't *you* going?" Ridge asked, looking even more disgruntled.

"I'm planning to sit this one out. I have court tomorrow and some work to do before then. And, to be honest, I'm not sure being bounced around on a hay wagon right now would be the best thing for, well, for the baby."

For a moment everyone stared at her. Even the girls who had come for Gabi's little sleigh ride party stopped their giggly chatter.

"Baby? You're having a baby?" Laura exclaimed.

Becca nodded and Trace hugged her more tightly, then kissed the top of her head, clearly a proud papa.

"When?" Caidy asked, thrilled for both of them.

"June," Gabi declared proudly. "I've been *dying* to tell everyone! I kept my mouth shut, see, Trace? You said I couldn't. Ha!"

Her brother laughed and grabbed his wife's sister with his free arm, pulling her into their shared embrace. "You did good, kid. We were going to tell everyone at dinner but the right moment never quite came."

"There's never a *wrong* moment for that kind of great news," Ridge said. "Congratulations. Another Bowman. Just what the world needs."

The next few moments were spent with hugs and kisses and good wishes all the way around. Even Ben shook both of their hands and kissed Becca's cheek, though he had just met her that afternoon.

She suddenly remembered with a pang that he had lost a child when his wife died. Was this spontaneous celebration of impending parenthood difficult for him? If it was, he didn't show it by his manner.

Now Maya's chant changed to "baby, baby, baby," but she didn't lose the hip wiggle. Caidy hugged her too. "It's wonderful news, isn't it? You'll have a new cousin."

"I like cousins," Maya said.

"Me too, bug."

When Caidy finally worked her way around the crowd, she hugged Becca. "I can't wait to be an aunt again. I'm thrilled for both of you."

Becca hugged her back. "Thank you, my dear."

"All the more reason I should stay here and keep you company, just in case you need anything."

Becca gave her a knowing look. "You're the soul of

helpfulness, Caidy. Either that, or you're trying to avoid a certain rude, arrogant veterinarian."

She cringed at the reminder. "Well, there is that."

"Sorry, hon. I'd like to help you out but I think Ridge probably needs your help corralling all those kids. Besides that, I don't think it's a good idea to keep avoiding him."

"Am I that obvious?" she asked ruefully.

"A little bit. Probably Laura and I were the only ones who picked up on it. And maybe Ben."

Caidy blew out a breath. Drat. Becca was right. Ridge probably *did* need her help. "I hate being a coward," she murmured.

"It's only a sleigh ride. An hour out of your life. You can handle that. You've been through much worse."

"I don't want to leave you."

"I could use a little quiet, if you want the truth. Go, Caidy."

"As exciting as this news is, we need to get this show on the road," Ridge declared, as if on cue. "Let's load up."

The girls squealed loudly. Maya covered her ears with her mittened hands, wearing a look of alarm.

Caidy gave her a reassuring smile. "Don't worry about those silly girls. They just want to go have fun."

"Me too. You come."

She sighed, resigned to her fate. "Yes, Queen Maya."

The girl gave her sweet giggle as Caidy grabbed her coat out of the closet and quickly found mittens and a quite fancy chapeau handmade by Emery Kendall Cavazos that she had won in the gift exchange a few weeks earlier at the Friends of the Library Christmas party.

"Hurry up, Caid," Taft said. "We don't have all night.

The sooner we go, the sooner we can get it over with and come back to watch the basketball game. Come on, Maya."

"I stay with Auntie," the girl said and Caidy's heart melted, as it frequently did around her.

"I've got her," she told her brother.

"Are you sure?"

"Yes. We're coming. I'm almost ready."

Taft left and she quickly finished shoving on boots, grabbed Maya's hand and hurried out to the hay wagon.

The horses stamped and blew in the cold air, which smelled of woodsmoke and snow. What a beautiful night. Perfect for a sleigh ride. Well, not officially a sleigh ride because the wagon had wheels, not runners, but she didn't think any of them would quibble.

Ridge had lined the wagon with straw bales. To her dismay, everyone else was settling as they approached the wagon and the only free space left for her and Maya was near the back of the wagon—right next to Ben. Had her brothers colluded to arrange that? She wouldn't put it past them.

Right now, Ben was more likely to throw her over the side than cooperate with any Bowman matchmaking efforts, but her brothers had no way of knowing that— unless Laura or Becca had spilled to their husbands.

"Auntie, up," Maya said.

How was she going to manage this? Maya wasn't heavy but Caidy didn't think she could climb the ladder with her in her arms and she wasn't sure Maya could negotiate them on her own. "If you want to lift her up, I can help her the rest of the way," Ben said, obviously noticing her predicament.

Caidy scooped Maya into her arms and held her up for him. Their arms brushed as he easily tugged the girl the rest of the way. Did he feel the sparks between them, or was it just her imagination? Caidy climbed the ladder and stood for a moment, wishing she could squeeze up front with Ridge. Unfortunately, he already had Alex and Jack riding shotgun.

"Sit down, Caidy, or you're going to fall over when Ridge takes off," Taft ordered. Heaven save her from brothers who didn't think she had a brain in her head.

Left with no choice, she sat on the same bale as Ben—who looked rugged and masculine in a fleece-lined heavy ranch coat the color of dust. At least Maya sat between them, providing some buffer.

Ridge turned around to make sure all his passengers were settled and then clicked to the big horses. They took off down the driveway, accompanied by the jangle of bells on the harnesses.

"Go, horsies! Jingle bells, jingle bells!" Maya exclaimed and Caidy smiled at her. When she lifted her gaze, she found Ben smiling down at the girl too. Her heart stuttered a little at the gentleness on his expression. She had called him rude and arrogant, yet here he was treating Maya, with her beautiful smile and Down syndrome features, with breathtaking sweetness.

She had to say something. Now was the perfect time. She clenched her fingers into her palms inside her mittens and turned to him. "Look, I…I'm sorry about earlier. What I said. It wasn't true. Not any of it. I was just being stupid."

"What?" he yelled, leaning down to hear over the rushing wind and the eight laughing girls.

"I said I'm sorry." She spoke more loudly but at that moment all the girls started actually singing "Jingle Bells" in time with the chiming bells from the horses.

"What?" He leaned his head closer to hers, over

Maya's head, and she didn't know what else to do but lean in and speak in his ear, though she felt completely ridiculous. She wanted to tell him to just forget the whole thing. She had come this far, though. She might as well finish the thing.

Up close, he smelled delicious. She couldn't help noticing that outdoorsy soap she had noticed when they were kissing....

She dragged her mind away from that and focused on the apology she should be making. "I said I was sorry," she said in his ear. "For what I said in the kitchen to my sisters-in-law, I mean. They were teasing me, uh, about you...and I was being completely stupid. I'm sorry you overheard. I didn't mean it."

He turned his head until his face was only inches from hers. "Any of it?"

"Well, you are pretty arrogant," she answered tartly.

To her surprise, he laughed at that and the low, sexy timbre of it shivered down her spine and spread out her shoulders to her fingertips.

"I can be," he answered.

"Sing!" Maya commanded as the girls broke into "Rudolph the Red-Nosed Reindeer."

She laughed and picked the girl onto her lap, grateful for her small, warm weight and the distraction she provided from this very inconvenient attraction she didn't know what to do about to a man who was sending her more mixed signals than a broken traffic light.

She was taken further off guard when Ben began to sing along with Maya and the girls in a very pleasing tenor. He even sang all the extra lines about lightbulbs and reindeers playing Monopoly.

She had to turn away, focusing instead on the homes

they passed, their holiday lights glittering in the pale moonlight.

This wasn't such a bad way to spend an evening, she decided. Even with the caroling, she was surrounded by family she loved, by beautiful scenery, by the serenity of a winter night. She was happy she had come, she realized with some shock.

The girls broke into "Silent Night" after that, changing up the lighthearted mood a little, and she hummed softly under her breath while Maya mangled the words but did her best to follow along. In the middle of the first "Sleep in heavenly peace" injunction, Ben leaned down once more.

"Why aren't you singing?" His low voice tickled her ear and gave her chills underneath the layers of wool.

She shrugged, unable to answer him. She wasn't sure she could tell him at all and she certainly couldn't tell him on a jangly, noisy sleigh ride surrounded by family and Destry's friends.

"Seriously," he pressed, leaning away when the song ended and they could converse a little more easily. "Do you have some ideological or religious objection to Christmas songs I should know about?"

She shook her head. "No. I just…don't sing."

"Don't listen to her," Taft said. She must have spoken louder than she intended if her brother could overhear from the row of hay bales ahead of them.

"Caidy has a beautiful voice," he went on. "She used to sing solos in the school and church choir. Once she even sang the national anthem by herself at a high school football game."

Goodness. She barely remembered that. How did Taft? He had been a wildlands firefighter when she was in high school, traveling across the West with an elite smoke-jumper squad, but she now recalled he had been home visiting Laura and had come to hear her sing at that football game.

He was the only one of her brothers who had been able to make it. Ridge had still been feuding with their father and had been living on a ranch in Montana and Trace had been deployed in the Middle East.

She suddenly remembered how freaked she had been as she walked out to take the microphone and had seen the huge hometown crowd gathered there, just about everybody she knew. Despite all her hours of practice with her voice teacher and the choir director, panic had spurted through her and she completely forgot the opening words—until she looked up in the stands and saw her mother and father beaming at her and Taft and Laura giving her an encouraging wave. A steady calm had washed over her like water from the irrigation canals, washing away all the panic, and she had sung beautifully. Probably the best performance of her life.

Just a few months later, her parents were dead because of her and all the songs inside her had died with them.

"I don't sing *anymore*," she said, hoping that would be the end of it. She didn't want to answer the question. It was nobody's business but her own—certainly not Ben Caldwell's.

He gave her a long look. The wagon jolted over a rut in the road and his shoulder bumped hers. She could have eased far enough away that they wouldn't touch but she didn't. Instead, she rested her cheek on Maya's hair, humming along with "O Little Town of Bethlehem" and gazing up at the few stars revealed through the wispy clouds as she waited for the ride to be over.

* * *

He sensed a story here.

Something was up with the Bowmans when it came to Christmas. He noticed that while Laura and the children were singing merrily away, Caidy's brothers seemed as reluctant as she to join in. The police chief and fire chief would occasionally sing a few lines and Caidy hummed here and there, but none of them could be called enthusiastic participants in this little sing-along.

At random moments over the evening he had picked up a pensive, almost sad mood threading through their family.

He thought of that beautiful work of art in the dining room, the vibrant colors and the intense passion behind it, and then the way all the Bowmans shut down as if somebody had yanked a window screen closed when he had asked about the artist.

Their mother. What happened to her? And the father was obviously gone too. He was intensely curious but didn't know how to ask.

The three-quarter moon peeked behind a cloud, and in the pale moonlight she was almost breathtakingly lovely, with those delicate features and that soft, very kissable mouth.

That kiss hadn't been far from his mind all day, probably because he still didn't quite understand what had happened. He wasn't the kind of man to steal a kiss from a beautiful woman, especially not at the spur of the moment like that. But he hadn't been able to resist her. She had looked so sweet and lovely there in her kitchen, worry for her ailing dog still a shadow in her eyes.

Holding her in his arms, he had desired her, of course, but had also been aware of something else tangled with the hunger, a completely unexpected tenderness. He sensed she used her prickly edges as a defense against the world, keeping away potential threats before they could get too close.

He remembered her cutting words to her brothers' wives and that awkward moment when he had walked into the kitchen just in time to hear her call him arrogant and rude.

Why hadn't he just slipped out of the kitchen again without any of the women suspecting he might have overheard? He should have. It would have been the polite thing to do, but some demon had prompted him to push her, to let her know he wasn't about to be dismissed so easily.

She had apologized for it, said she hadn't meant any of her words. So why had she said them?

He made her nervous. He had observed at dinner that she was warm and friendly to everyone else, but she basically ignored him and had been abrupt in their few interactions. It was an odd position in which to find himself and he wasn't sure how he felt about it—just as he didn't know how to deal with his own conflicted reaction to her.

One moment he wanted to retreat into his safe world as a widower and single father. The next, she forcibly reminded him that underneath those roles, he was still a man.

Brooke had been gone for two years. He would always grieve for his wife, for the good times they had shared and the children she had loved and raised so well. He had become, if not complacent in his grief, at least comfortable with it. This move to Idaho seemed to have shaken everything. When he agreed to take the job, he intended to create a new life for the children, away from influences he considered harmful. He never expected to find himself so drawn to a lovely woman with secrets and sadness in her eyes.

Through the rest of the sleigh ride, though he tried to focus on the scenery and the enjoyment his children were having, he couldn't seem to stop watching Caidy. She was amazing, actually, keeping her attention focused on entertaining the very cute niece on her lap and making sure none of the gaggle of preadolescent girls suddenly fell out of the wagon. She managed all of those tasks with deft skill.

She obviously loved children and she was very good with them. Why didn't she have a husband and a wagonload of children herself?

None of his business, he reminded himself. Her dog was his patient and he was currently a temporary tenant at her ranch, but that was the extent of their relationship. He would be foolish to go looking for more. That didn't stop him from being intensely aware of her as the wagon jostled his shoulder against hers every time Ridge hit a rut.

"Brrr. I'm cold," Maya said, snuggling deeper into Caidy's lap.

"So am I," she answered. "But look. Ridge is taking us home now."

Ben looked around. Sure enough, her brother had perfect timing. Just as the enthusiasm began to wane and the children started to complain of the cold, Ben realized the big, beautiful draft horses were trudging under the sign announcing the entrance to the River Bow Ranch.

"No more horsies?" Maya asked.

"Not today, little bug." Taft held his arms out and his

stepdaughter lunged into them. "We'll come back and go for another ride sometime soon, though, I promise."

"She's a huge fan of our horses," Caidy said with a fond smile for the girl. "Especially the big ones for some odd reason."

Instead of heading toward the ranch house, Caidy's brother turned the horses down the little lane that led to the house he was renting. The wagon pulled up in front.

"Look at that. Curb service for you," Caidy said. She finally met his gaze with a tentative smile. He was aware of an unsettling urge to stand here in the cold, staring into those striking green eyes for an hour or two. He managed a brief smile in return, then turned his attention to climbing out of the wagon and gathering his kids.

"Let's go. Jack, Ava."

"I don't want to get off! Why does everyone else get to keep riding?" Jack had that tremor in his voice that signaled an impending five-year-old tantrum.

"Only for another minute or two," Ridge promised. "We're just heading back to the house and then the ride will be done. The horses are tired and need their beds."

"So do you, kiddo," Ben said. "Come on."

To Ben's relief, Jack complied, jumping down into his arms. Ava clearly wanted to stay with the other girls but she finally waved to them all. "See you tomorrow on the bus," she said to Destry.

"Great. I'll bring that book we were talking about."

"Okay. Don't forget."

Ava waved again and jumped down without his help.

"Thanks for letting us tag along," he said to the wagon in general, though he meant his words for Caidy. "Ava and Jack had a blast."

"What about you?" she asked.

He didn't know her well enough yet to interpret her moods. All he knew was that she looked remarkably pretty in the moonlight, with her eyes sparkling and her cheeks—and the very tip of her nose—rosy.

"I enjoyed it," he answered. He was a little surprised to realize it was true. He hadn't found all that many things enjoyable since his wife died. Who would have expected he would enjoy a hayride with a bunch of giggly girls and Caidy and her forbidding brothers, who would probably have thrown him off the wagon if they had known about that late-night kiss—and about how very much he wanted to repeat the experience?

"I especially enjoyed the peppermint hot cocoa."

She looked pleased. "I'm glad. Peppermint is my favorite too."

"Good night."

He waved and carried Jack into the foreman's cottage, wondering what the hell he was going to do about Caidy Bowman. She was an intriguing mystery, a jumble full of prickles and sweetness, vinegar and sugar, and he was far more fascinated by her than he had any right to be.

Chapter Ten

After the sleigh ride, Caidy made it a point for the next few days to stay as far as possible from the foreman's house. She had no reason to visit. Why would she? Ben and the children and Mrs. Michaels were perfectly settled and didn't need help with anything.

If she stood at her bedroom window, looking out at the night and the sparkling lights nestled among the trees, well, that was her own business. She told herself she was only enjoying the peace and serenity of these quiet December nights, but that didn't completely explain away the restlessness that seemed to ache inside her.

It certainly had nothing to do with a certain dark-haired man and the jittery butterflies he sent dancing around inside her.

She couldn't hope to avoid him forever, though. On Wednesday, less than a week before Christmas, she woke from tangled dreams with an odd sense of trepidation.

The vague sense of unease dogged her heels like a blurred shadow as she headed out to the barn with a still-sleepy Destry to feed and water the horses and take care of the rest of their chores.

She couldn't figure it out until they finished in the barn and headed back to the welcoming warmth of the house for breakfast before the school bus came. When they walked into the kitchen, they were greeted by a happy bark from the crate she had returned to the corner and she suddenly remembered.

This was the day she had to take Luke back to the veterinarian to have his wound checked and his stitches removed. She stopped stock-still in the kitchen, trepidation pressing down on her. Drat. She couldn't avoid the man forever, she supposed. A few more days would be nice, though. Was it too late to make an appointment with the vet in Idaho Falls?

"What's wrong?" Destry asked. "Your face looks funny. Did you see a mouse?"

She raised an eyebrow. "In my kitchen? Are you kidding me? I better not. No. I just remembered something…unpleasant."

"Reverend Johnson said in Sunday school that the best way to get rid of bad thoughts is to replace them by thinking about something good."

The girl measured dry oatmeal into her bowl and reached for the teakettle Caidy always turned on before they headed out to the barn. "I've been trying to do that whenever I think about my mom," she said casually.

Thoughts of Ben flew out the window as she stared at her niece. Destry *never* talked about her mother. In recent memory, Caidy could only recall a handful of times when Melinda's name even came up. Destry was so sweet and even-tempered, and Ridge was such an attentive father, she had just assumed the girl had adjusted to losing her mother, but she supposed no child ever completely recovered from that loss, whether she was three at the time or sixteen.

"Does that happen often?" she asked carefully. She didn't want to cut off the line of dialogue if Destry wanted to open up. "Thinking about your mother, I mean?"

Destry shrugged and added an extra spoonful of brown sugar to her oatmeal. Caidy decided to let it slide for once. "Not really. I can hardly remember her, you know? But I still wonder about her, especially at Christmas. I don't even know if she's dead or alive. Gabi at least knows her mom is alive—she's just being a big jerk."

Jerk was a kind word for the mother of both Gabi and Becca. She was a first-class bitch, selfish and irresponsible, who had given both of her daughters childhoods filled with uncertainty and turmoil.

"Have you asked your dad about…your mother?"

"No. He doesn't like to talk about her much." Destry paused, a spoonful of steaming oatmeal halfway between the bowl and her mouth. "I really don't remember much about her. I was so little when she left. She wasn't very nice, was she?"

Another kind phrase. Melinda showed up in a thesaurus as the antonym to nice. She had fooled them all in the beginning, especially Ridge. She had seemed sweet and rather needy and hopelessly in love with him, but time—or perhaps her own natural temperament—had showed a different side of her. By the time she finally left River Bow, just about all of them had been relieved to see her go.

"She was…troubled." Caidy picked through her words with caution. "I don't think she had a very happy life when she was your age. Sometimes those bad things in the past can make it tough for a person to see all the good things they have now. I'm afraid that was your mother's problem."

Destry appeared to ponder that as she took another spoonful of oatmeal. "It stinks, doesn't it?" she said quietly after a long moment. "I don't think I could ever leave my kid, no matter what."

Her heart ached for this girl and for inexplicable truths. "Neither could I. And yes, you're right. It does stink. She made some poor choices. Unfortunately, you've had to suffer for those. But you need to look at the good things you have. Your dad didn't go anywhere. He loves you more than anything and he's been here the whole time showing you that. I'm here and the twins and now their families. You have lots and lots of people who love you, Des. If your mom couldn't see how wonderful you are, that's her problem—not yours. Don't ever forget that."

"I know. I remember. Most of the time anyway."

Caidy leaned over and hugged her niece. Des rested her head on her shoulder for just a moment before she returned to her breakfast with her usual equanimity.

Caidy wasn't the girl's mother, but she thought she was doing a pretty good job as a surrogate. Worlds better than Melinda would have done, if Caidy did say so herself.

After Destry finished breakfast and helped her clean up the dishes, Caidy had just enough time to spare to run her the quarter mile from the house to the bus stop.

"Ava and Jack aren't here," her niece fretted. "Do you think they forgot what time the bus comes? Maybe we should have picked them up."

"I'm sure Mrs. Michaels knows what time the bus comes," she answered. "They've been here the past few days in plenty of time, haven't they? Maybe they just caught a ride with their father today."

"Maybe," Destry said, though she still looked worried.

Caidy could have given Des a ride into town this morning on her way to the vet, she realized. She hadn't even thought about that until right now—just as the school bus lumbered over the hill and stopped in front of them with a screech of air brakes.

After Destry climbed on the bus and Caidy waved her off, she hurried back to the house and carried the dog crate out to the ranch's Suburban, then returned for the dog, who was moving around much more comfortably these days.

"Luke, buddy, you're not making things easy on me. If not for you, I could pretend the man doesn't exist."

The dog tilted his head and gazed at her with an expression that looked almost apologetic. She laughed a little and hooked up his leash before leading him carefully out to the Suburban, where she lifted him carefully into the crate.

Maybe Ridge could take him into the vet for her.

The fleeting thought was far too tempting. As much as she wanted to ask him for the favor, she knew she couldn't. This was all part of her ongoing effort to prove to herself she wasn't a complete coward.

For a brief instant as she slid behind the wheel, a random image flitted through her memory—cowering under that shelf in the pantry, gazing at the ribbon of light streaming in under the door and listening to the squelchy sounds of her mother's breathing.

She pushed away the memories.

Oh, how she loathed Christmas.

She was in a lousy mood when she pulled up in front of the vet clinic, a combination of her worry over Destry missing her mother and missing her *own* mother, not to mention her reluctance to walk inside that building and face Ben again after all the awkwardness between them.

This was ridiculous. She frowned at herself. She was tough enough to go on roundup every year to get their cattle from the high mountain grazing allotment. She helped Ridge with branding and with breaking new horses and even with castrating steers.

Surely she was tough enough to endure a fifteen-minute checkup with the veterinarian, no matter how sexy the dratted man was.

With that resolve firmly in mind, she moved around to the back of the Suburban with Luke's leash. Border collies were ferociously smart, though, and he clearly was even more reluctant than she to go inside the building. He fought the leash, wriggling his head this way and that and trying to scramble as far back as he could into the crate.

She imagined this building represented discomfort and fear to him. She could completely understand that, but that didn't change the fact that he would have to suck it up and go inside anyway.

If she did, he did.

"Come on, Luke. Easy now. There's a boy. Come on."

"Problem?"

Her heart kicked up a beat at the familiar voice. She turned with an air of trepidation and there he was in all his gorgeousness. A flood of heat washed over her, seeping into all the cold corners.

"You've got a reluctant patient here." *And his reluctant person.*

"A common problem in my line of work. I saw you from the window and thought it might be something like that."

"I didn't want to yank him out for fear of hurting something."

He gestured to the crate. "May I?"

"Of course."

She moved out of the way and he stepped forward, leaning down to the opening of the crate. She tried not to notice the way the morning sunshine gleamed in his dark hair or the breadth of those shoulders under his blue scrubs.

She was beginning to find it extremely unfair that the only man to rev her engine in, well, ever, was somebody who was obviously not interested in a relationship. At least with her.

"Hey there, Luke. How's my bud?" He spoke in a low, calm voice that sent shivers down her spine. If he ever turned that voice on *her,* she would turn into a quivery mass of hormones.

"You want to come inside? There's a good boy. Come on. Yeah. Nothing to worry about here."

As she watched, Luke surrendered to the spell of that gentle voice and stood docile while Ben hooked on the leash and carefully lifted the dog down to the snowy ground.

"He's moving well. That's a good sign."

Luke promptly lifted a leg against the tire of the Suburban, just in case any other creatures around wondered to whom it might belong. Ben didn't seem fazed.

No doubt that also was a natural occurrence in his line of work.

After Luke finished, Ben led them to the side door she had used so many times when she worked for Doc Harris. "Let's just head straight to the exam room. I had a break between patients this morning and I'm all ready for you. We can take care of the paperwork afterward."

He closed the door and she immediately wondered how such an ordinary act could completely deplete all available oxygen. Being alone with him in this enclosed space left her breathless, off balance and painfully aware of him.

She sank into a chair while he started his exam of the dog. The whole time she tried to ignore that low, calming voice and his easy, comfortable manner with the animal, focusing instead on her mental to-do list before Christmas Eve, which was in less than a week.

"Everything looks good," Ben finally said. "He's progressing much more quickly than I expected."

"Great news. Thank you."

"If it's all right with you, I'd like to leave the stitches in for a few more days. I'll try to stop by over the holidays to remove them."

"I don't want you to go to so much trouble. I can probably remove them. I've done it before."

He raised an eyebrow. "You *have* had experience at this."

She shrugged. "Most everybody who grows up on a ranch gets basic veterinary experience. It's part of the life. I took it a little further when I worked with Doc Harris, that's all."

"If you ever want another job, I could use an experienced tech."

Oh, wouldn't that be a disaster? She couldn't think

straight around the man. She could only imagine what sort of mess she could create trying to help him in a professional capacity.

"I'll keep that in mind."

"Actually, I do need a favor. Advice, really. You know just about everybody in town, don't you?"

"Most of them. We've had some new people move in lately but I'm sure I'll get around to meeting them."

"Do you know any after-school babysitters?"

"Is something wrong with Mrs. Michaels?" she asked, concerned all over again about the children not making it to the bus stop that morning.

His sigh was heavy. "No. Not with her, but she has a married daughter in California who just had a baby."

"Oh, that's great. I remember you mentioned her daughter was expecting."

"She wasn't due for another month, but apparently she went into premature labor yesterday and had the baby this morning. The baby is in the newborn ICU. Anne wants to be there, which I completely get. She's trying to make arrangements to fly out today so she can be there when her daughter comes home from the hospital, and then she plans to stay through the holidays."

"Understandable."

"I know. I do understand, believe me. It just makes *my* life a little more complicated right now, at least temporarily. The children can always come here after school. I don't mind having them. But according to Ava, hanging out at the clinic is 'totally boring.' Plus Jack can usually find trouble wherever he goes, a skill that sometimes can be a little inconvenient at a clinic filled with ailing animals."

"I can see where that might pose a problem."

"I need to find someone for this Saturday at least.

We have clinic appointments all day because of our shortened holiday hours next week and I don't feel right about sticking them here for ten hours."

Against her will, she felt a pang of sympathy for the man. It couldn't have been easy, moving to Pine Gulch where he didn't know anyone. He and his children had left behind any kind of support network, all trace of the familiar. Starting over in a new community would be tough on anyone, especially a single father also trying to keep a demanding business operating.

"This is easily fixed, Ben," she said impulsively. "Ava and Jack can come to the ranch house after school and hang out with me and Destry. It will be great fun."

He looked faintly embarrassed. "That wasn't a hint, I swear. I honestly never even thought about asking you. Because you know everyone in town and all, I thought you might be aware of someone who might be willing to help out this time of year."

"I do know a few people who do childcare. I can certainly give you some names, if that's your preference. But I promise, having them come to the ranch after school would be no big deal. Destry would love the company and I might even put them to work with chores. They can ride the bus home with Destry the rest of the week, just like they would if Mrs. Michaels were there. Saturday's no problem either. Des and I are making Christmas cookies and can always use a couple more hands."

He shifted. "I don't want to bother you. I'm sure you're busy with Christmas."

"Who isn't? Don't worry about it, Ben. If I thought it would be too much of a bother, I wouldn't have offered."

"I don't know."

He was plainly reluctant to accept the help. Stubborn

man. Did he think she was going to attach strings to her offer? One kiss per hour of childcare?

Tempting. Definitely tempting…

"I was only trying to help. I thought it would be a convenient solution to your problem with the side benefit of helping me keep Destry entertained in the big crazy lead-up to Christmas Eve, but it won't hurt my feelings if you prefer to make other arrangements. You can think about it and let me know."

"I don't need to think about it. You're right. It is the perfect solution." He was quiet, his hands petting Luke's fur. Lucky dog.

"It's tough for me to accept help," he finally said, surprising her with his raw honesty. "Tougher, probably, to accept help from *you,* with things so…complicated between us."

"Complicated. Is that what you call it?" Apparently she wasn't the only one in tumult over this attraction that simmered between them.

"What word would you use?"

Tense. Sparkly. Exhilarating. She couldn't use any of those words, despite the truth of them.

"Complicated works, I guess. But this, at least, is relatively easy when you think about it. I like your kids, Ben. I don't mind having them around. Jack has a hilarious sense of humor and I'm sure he'll talk my ear off with knock-knock jokes. Ava is a little tougher nut to crack, I'll admit, but I'm looking forward to the challenge."

"She's struggling right now. I guess that's obvious."

"The move?"

"She's angry about that. About everything. My former in-laws did a number on her. They blame me for Brooke's death and have spent the past two years trying to shove a wedge between Ava and me. Both kids, really, but Jack is still too young to pay them much attention."

"Do they have any real reason to blame you?" she asked.

"They think they do. Brooke had type 1 diabetes and nearly died having Jack. The doctors told us not to try again. She was determined to have a third child despite the danger. She could be like that. If she wanted something, she couldn't see any reason why she couldn't have it. I wasn't about to risk a pregnancy. We took double precautions—or at least I thought I did. I intended to make things permanent, but the day I was scheduled for the big snip, she told me she was pregnant."

"Oh, no."

He raked a hand through his hair with a grimace. "Why am I compelled to spill all this to you?"

She chose her words with Ben as carefully as she had with Destry earlier, sensing if she said the wrong thing to him this fragile connection between them would fray. "I would like to think we can be friends, even if things between us are…complicated."

He gave a rough laugh. "Friends. All right. I guess I don't have enough of those around."

She sensed that wasn't an admission he was comfortable with either. "You will. Give it time. You just moved in. It takes time to build that kind of trust."

"Even with my friends back in California, I never felt right about talking about this. It sounds terrible of me. Disloyal or something. I loved my wife but…some part of me is so damn angry at her. She got pregnant on purpose. I guess that's obvious. She stopped taking birth control pills and sabotaged the condoms. She thought she knew better than the doctors and me."

What kind of mother risked her life, her future with a husband who loved her and children who needed her, simply because she wanted something she didn't have? Caidy couldn't conceive of it.

"I loved her but she could be stubborn and spoiled when she wanted her way. She wouldn't consider terminating the pregnancy despite the dangers," Ben went on. Now that he had started with the story, she sensed he wanted to tell her all of it. "For several months, things were going well. We thought anyway. Then when she was six months along, her glucose levels started jumping all over the place. As best we can figure out, it must have spiked that afternoon and she passed out."

His hands curled in Luke's fur. "She was behind the wheel at the time and drove off an overpass. She and the baby both died instantly."

"Oh, Ben. I'm so sorry." She wanted to touch him, offer some sort of comfort, but she was afraid to move. What would he do if she wrapped her fingers around his? Friends did that sort of thing, right? Even complicated friends?

"Her parents never forgave me." He spoke before she could move. "They thought it was all my fault she got pregnant in the first place. If only I'd stayed away from her, et cetera, et cetera. I can't really blame them."

She stared. "I can. That's completely ridiculous. Are they nuts? You were married, for heaven's sake. What were you supposed to do? It's not like you were two teenagers having a quickie in the backseat of your car."

He gave a rough, surprised-sounding laugh, and she was aware of a tiny bubble of happiness inside her that she could make him laugh despite the grim story.

"You're right. They are a little nuts." He laughed again and some of the tension in his shoulders started to ease. "No, a *lot* nuts. That's the real reason I moved here. Ava was becoming just like my mother-in-law. A little carbon copy, right down to the tight-mouthed expressions and the censorious comments. I won't let that happen. I'm her father and I'm not about to let them feed her lies and distortions until she hates me."

"Is the move working the way you hoped?"

"I think it's too soon to tell. She's still pretty upset at moving away from them. They can give her things I can't. That's a tough thing for a father to stomach."

This time she acted on the impulse to touch him and rested a hand on his bare forearm, just below the short sleeve of the scrub shirt. His skin was warm, the muscle hard beneath her fingers.

"They can't give either Ava or Jack the most important thing. Your love. That's what they're going to remember the rest of their lives. When they see how much you have loved them and sacrificed for them, it won't matter what lies their grandparents try to feed them."

"Thank you for that." He smiled at her, his eyes crinkling a little at the corners, and she wanted to stand in this little office basking in the glow forever.

Why, again, hadn't she wanted to bring Luke to the vet? She couldn't imagine anywhere she would rather be right now.

"I mean it about the kids, Ben." Though it took a great deal of effort, she managed to slide her hand away. "Destry and I would love to have the children hang out with us for a few days. And if you need help between Christmas and New Year's, we'll be happy to keep an eye on them."

The conviction in her voice seemed to assuage the last of his concerns. "If you're sure, that would be great. Thank you. You've lifted a huge weight off my mind."

"No problem." She smiled to seal the deal. His gaze flickered to her mouth and stayed there as if he couldn't look away. He was thinking of their kiss. She was certain of it. Awareness fluttered through her, low and enticing. When his gaze lifted to hers, she knew she wasn't imagining the sudden hunger there.

She swallowed, her face suddenly hot. She wanted him to kiss her again, just wrap his arms around her and press her back against the wall for the next hour or two.

Not the time or the place. He was working and had other patients he needed to see. Besides that, though he might be forging this tentative friendship with her, she had a feeling the rest of it was just too tangled for either of them right now.

"I'll, um, see you later," she mumbled. "Thanks for… everything."

"You're very welcome." His low voice thrummed over her nerves. She did her best to ignore it as she grabbed the end of Luke's leash and escaped.

Chapter Eleven

Two nights later, Ben pulled off the main road onto the drive into the River Bow, wishing he could hang a left at the junction, climb into his bed at the cottage and sleep for the next two or three days.

His shoulders were tight with exhaustion, his eyes gritty and aching. When he finally found time to sleep, just past midnight, he had only been under for a few minutes when he received an emergency call to help a dog that had been hit by a car on one of the ranch roads. He had ended up packing his sleepy kids—poor things—into the backseat of the SUV and taking them inside his office to sleep while he attended to the dog.

He really needed Mrs. Michaels—or someone like her. At least the kids had fallen quickly back to sleep. He considered that a great blessing. Even after he packed them back to the ranch and into their beds, they had again fallen asleep easily.

He had envied them that as he tossed and turned, energized by the case and the successful outcome. Before he knew it, the alarm was going off and he had stumbled out of bed to face a packed schedule of people rushing to take their animals into the vet before the clinic went on its brief holiday hiatus.

So far, he hadn't seen any slowdown in business after taking over from Dr. Harris. Another blessing there. Although he was grateful for the business and glad that the people of Pine Gulch had decided to continue bringing their animals to him, right now he was too tired to savor his relief.

As he pulled up to the River Bow ranch house, Christmas lights gleamed against the winter night and the darker silhouettes of the mountains in the distance and the pines and aspens of the foreground. Warm light spilled out the windows into the snow and that big Christmas tree twinkled with color.

The place offered a cheery welcome against the chilly night. He couldn't help thinking about his grandparents' home in Lake Forest. In sheer square footage, Caldwell House was probably three times as big as the River Bow, but instead of warmth and hominess, he remembered his childhood home as being sterile and unfriendly to a young boy, all sharp angles, dark wood and uncomfortable furniture.

His grandparents hadn't wanted him. He had known that from the beginning when their daughter, his mother, had dropped him and his sister off before running off with her latest hard-living boyfriend.

She hadn't come back, of course. Even at age eight, he had somehow known she wouldn't. Now he knew she had died of a drug overdose just months after dropping him and Susie with her parents, but for years he had watched and waited for a mother who would never return.

Oh, his grandparents had done their duty. They had given him and Susie a roof over their head, nutritious meals, an excellent education. But he and his sister had never been allowed to forget they came from a selfish, irresponsible woman who had chosen drugs over her own children.

He had his own family now. Children he loved more than anything. He would never treat them as unwanted burdens.

Eager to pick them up now, he pulled up in front of the River Bow. The night was clear and cold, with a brilliant spill of stars gleaming above the mountains. Inside the door, he could hear laughter and a television show, along with a couple of well-mannered barks.

The door opened just seconds after he rang the bell. His stomach rumbled instantly as the spicy, doughy smells wafting outside immediately transported him to his favorite pizzeria in college.

"Hi, Dad!" Jack let go of the doorknob just an instant before launching himself toward Ben. With a laugh, he held his arms out and Jack did his traditional move of spider-walking up his legs before Ben flipped him upside down, then scooped him up into his arms.

He always found it one of life's tiny miracles that his exhaustion could seep away for a while when he was reunited with his kids at the end of the day, even if Ava was in a cranky mood.

"How was your day, bud?"

"Great! I got to help feed the horses and play with some kittens. And guess what? I don't have to go back to school until next year."

"That's right. Last day of school and now it's Christmas vacation."

"And Santa Claus comes in *three days!*"

He had so dang much to do before then, Ben didn't even want to think about it. "I can't wait," he lied.

As he spoke, Ben became aware of what Jack would have called a disturbance in the Force. Some kind of shift in air currents or spinning and whirling of the ions in the air or something, he wasn't sure, but he sensed Caidy's approach even before she came into view.

"Hi! I thought I heard a doorbell."

She was wearing a white apron and had a bit of flour on her cheek, just a little dusting against her heat-flushed skin.

"Sorry I'm a little later than I told you I would be on the phone," he answered, fighting the urge to step forward and blow away the flour.

"No problem. We've been having fun, haven't we, Jack?"

"Yep. We're making pizza and I got to put some cheese on."

His stomach growled again and he realized he hadn't had time for lunch. "It smells great. Really great."

Jack grabbed one of his hands in both of his. "Can we stay and have some? Please, Dad!"

He glanced at Caidy, embarrassed that his son would offer invitations to someone else's meal. "I don't think so. I'm sure we've bothered the Bowmans long enough. We'll find something back at our place."

Exactly what, he wasn't quite sure. Maybe they would run into town to grab fast food, though right now loading up into the vehicle again and heading to the business district was the last thing he felt like doing. Maybe there was a pizza restaurant he hadn't discovered yet—because that smell was enticing.

"Of course you'll stay!" Caidy exclaimed. "I was planning on it."

"You're doing us enough favors by letting the kids come hang out with you. I don't expect you to feed us too."

She narrowed her gaze at him. "I just spent an hour making enough pizza dough to feed the whole town of Pine Gulch. You can stay a few minutes and eat a slice or two, can't you?"

He should make an excuse and leave. This house was just too appealing—and Caidy was even more so. But he didn't have plans for dinner. If they ate here, that was one less decision he would have to make. Besides, pizza on a cold winter night seemed perfect.

They could stay for a while, just long enough to eat, he decided. Then he and his children would head for home. "If you're sure, that would be great. It really does smell delicious."

"I'm going to be a lousy hostess and ask you to hang your own coat up because my hands are covered in flour, then come on back to the kitchen."

Without waiting for an answer, she turned around and walked back down the hall, Jack scampering after her. After a pause, Ben shrugged out of his ranch coat and hung it alongside Jack's and Ava's coats on the rack in the corner.

He expected to see a crowd of children when he walked into the kitchen but Caidy was alone. She tucked a strand of hair behind her ear, leaving another little smudge of flour, and gave him a bright smile that seemed to push off another shackle of his fatigue.

"The kids are just getting ready to watch a Christmas show in the other room. You're more than welcome to join them while I finish throwing things together in here."

He should. A wise man would take the escape she was handing him, but he didn't feel right about leaving her alone to do all the work. "Is there anything I can help you do in here?"

Surprise flickered in her eyes, then she smiled again. "You're a brave man, Ben Caldwell. Sure. I've got a cheese pizza cooking now to satisfy the restless natives. Give me a minute to toss out another pie and then you can put the toppings on."

He washed his hands, listening to the familiar opening strands of a holiday television special he had watched when *he* was a kid in the big rec room of Caldwell House. He found something rather comforting about the continuity of it, his own children enjoying the same things that had once given him pleasure.

"Would you like a drink or something? We don't keep much in the house but I can probably rustle up a beer."

"What are you having?"

"I like root beer with my pizza. It's always been kind of a family tradition and I apparently haven't grown out of it. Silly, isn't it?"

"I think it's nice. Root beer sounds good, but I can wait until the pizza is done."

She smiled as her hands expertly continued tossing the dough into shape. "What about you? Any traditions in the Caldwell family kitchen?"

"Other than thoroughly enjoying whatever Mrs. Michaels fixes us, no. Not really."

"What about when you were a kid?"

Traditions? No, not unless she might count formal

family dinners with little conversation and a serious dearth of kindness. "Not really. I didn't come from a particularly close family."

"No brothers or sisters?"

"A sister. She's several years younger than I am. We've lost touch over the years."

Susan had rebelled against their grandparents by following in their mother's footsteps, burying her misery in drugs and alcohol. Last he heard, she was in her third stint at rehab to avoid a prison sentence.

"I can't imagine losing touch with my brothers." Sympathy turned Caidy's eyes an intense green. "They're my best friends. Laura and Becca are like sisters to me now too."

"You Bowmans seem a united front against the world."

"I guess so. It hasn't always been that way, but it's the now that counts, right?"

"Yes. You're very lucky."

She opened her mouth to speak, then appeared to think better of it. "I think this should be ready now."

With a twist of her wrist, she deftly tossed the dough onto a pizza peel sprinkled with cornmeal and crimped the edges before handing the whole peel to him with a flourish.

"Here you go. All yours."

"Uh." He stared helplessly at the naked pizza dough, not quite sure what she expected of him.

"You haven't done this before, have you?"

He gave a rough laugh. "No. But I can tell you by heart the phone number of about half a dozen great pizza places in California."

She shook her head and stepped closer to him, stirring the air with the scent of wildflowers, and suddenly he forgot all about being hungry for pizza. Now he was just hungry for her.

"Okay, I'll walk you through it this time. Next time you come over for Friday night pizza, though, you're on your own."

Next time. Whoever would have guessed those two words could hold so much promise? He knew darn well he shouldn't feel this little kick of anticipation for something so nebulous and uncertain as a next time.

Better to just enjoy *this* moment. As she said, it was *now* that mattered. In a few weeks, he and his children would be moving away and Caidy Bowman and this wild attraction to her would be conveniently distant from him.

For now, she was here beside him, her skin unbelievably soft-looking and her hair teasing him with the scent of flowers and springtime.

"Okay, first thing you do is spoon a little sauce on. I like to use the bowl of the big spoon to spread it to the edge of the dough. That's it. Good."

He supposed it was fairly ridiculous to feel the same sense of pride in spreading sauce on a pizza dough as he had the first time he helped deliver a difficult foal.

"Now sprinkle as much cheese as you usually like. Perfect. I see you like it gooey."

She smiled at him and he suddenly wanted to toss the unfinished pizza to the floor, press her up against that counter and kiss her until they were both breathing hard.

"Okay, now put your toppings on. I was planning a pepperoni and olive for the next one but you can be creative. Whatever you think the kids might like."

"Pepperoni and olive sounds good." He cleared away the ragged edge to his voice. "My kids always like that."

She didn't appear to notice. "The third one can be a little more sophisticated. By then, Destry and her friends—and Ridge, when he's home—have had their fill."

Who made three homemade pizzas on a Friday night? Caidy Bowman apparently.

She was a woman of more layers than a supreme pizza and he was enjoying the process of uncovering each one.

"Now your toppings. Don't skimp on the olives."

He picked up a stack of pepperoni and dealt them like cards on poker night, then tossed handfuls of olives to the edge of the crust. This was going to be the best damn Friday night pizza she had ever had, he vowed.

"Okay, now another layer of cheese and then a bit of fresh Parmesan on the top. Oh, that looks delicious."

"Thank you."

"If the vet thing ever gets old, you can always get a job at the pizza place in town."

He laughed. "A backup plan is always helpful. Good to know I can still feed my kids."

She smiled back at him and he knew he didn't imagine it when her gaze flickered to his mouth and stayed there long enough to send heat pulsing through him. The moment stretched between them, heady and intoxicating, and he again wanted to kiss her, but she stepped away before he could act on the urge.

"I guess this one is ready."

"Now what?"

"Now I take the cheese pizza out, then we call in the locusts and watch it disappear."

He watched while she did just that, shoving a second pizza peel under the cooked pizza on a stone in the oven and deftly working the dough onto the peel before pulling the whole thing back out.

The cheese bubbled exactly the way he loved and the crust was golden perfection.

"Des!" she called. "The first pizza's ready. Can you pause the show and bring everybody in here?"

The herd of children galloped in a moment later, a few more than he expected. Ava was deep in conversation with Destry and Gabi while Jack was chattering away with Caidy's nephew, Alex, and niece Maya.

"Hi." Maya grinned at him in her adorable way and he couldn't help smiling back.

"Hi there."

"Did I mention I was babysitting Maya and Alex for a few hours tonight? Taft and Laura had some last-minute Christmas things to take care of. Laura's mom usually helps them out but she had a party tonight so I offered. I figured, what's a few more? And when Gabi heard Ava was coming over, of course she had to come too."

Now he understood why she was making so many pizzas.

Six kids. How did she handle it? He was overwhelmed most of the time with his own two, but Caidy seemed to juggle everything with ease. After transferring the other pizza from the peel to the stone in the oven, she poured drinks for the younger children, handed plates to the older girls and passed out napkins to everyone.

"Better grab a slice fast or it's going to be gone," she advised him. He snagged one of the few remaining pieces and a glass of frothy root beer and took a place at the kitchen table next to Jack.

All the children seemed ramped up for the holidays

but Caidy managed to keep them distracted by asking about the show they were watching, about their school parties that day, about what they wanted Santa to bring them.

He was too busy savoring the pizza to contribute much to the conversation but after the first blissful moments, he decided he had to try. "This is really delicious. I grew up in Chicago so I know pizza. The sauce is perfect."

"Thank you." She probably meant her pleased smile to be friendly and warm but he was completely seduced by it, by her, by this warm kitchen that seemed such a haven against the harsh, cold world outside.

"What about the third one? What's your pleasure?"

He could come up with several answers to that, none of them appropriate to voice with six children gathered around the table. "I don't really care. What's your favorite?"

"I like barbecue chicken. The kids generally tolerate it in moderation, so that only leaves more for me."

"I didn't realize you were such a devious woman, Caidy Bowman."

"I have my moments."

She smiled at him and he was struck by how lovely she was, with her dark hair escaping the ponytail and her cheeks flushed from the warmth of the stove.

He was in deep trouble here, he thought. He didn't know what to do about this attraction to her. He was hanging on with both hands to keep from falling hard for her, and each time he spent time with her, he slid down a few more inches.

"Do you know my dog?" Maya asked him earnestly. "His name is Lucky."

Grateful for the diversion, he shifted his gaze from

Caidy to her very adorable stepniece. "I don't think I've met Lucky yet. That's a very nice name for a dog."

"He *is* nice," Maya declared. "He licks my nose. It tickles."

"We have a dog named Tri," Jack announced.

"My dog's name is Grunt," Gabi said. "Trace says he's ugly but I think he's the most beautiful dog in the world."

"Lucky's beautiful too," Alex said. "He has super-long ears."

"Tri only has three legs," Jack said, as if that little fact trumped everything else.

"Cool!" Gabi said. "How does he get around?"

"He hops," Ava, who usually only barely tolerated the dog, piped in. "It's really kind of cute. He walks on his front two and then hops on the one back leg he's got. It takes *forever* to go on a walk with him, but I don't mind. Maya, you drank all your root beer. Do you want some more?"

Maya nodded and Ben smiled at his daughter as she poured a small amount of soda for the girl. All the children treated Maya with sweet consideration and it touched him, especially coming from Ava. Though she could be self-absorbed sometimes, like most children, she had these moments of kindness that heartened him.

"Here's pizza number two!" Caidy sang out to cheers from the children. While they had been talking about dogs, he had missed her pulling his pepperoni-and-olive creation out of the oven. Now she set it on the middle of the table and expertly sliced it. As before, the children each grabbed a slice. He nabbed a small one but noticed Caidy didn't take one.

"Want me to save you a piece? You'd better move fast."

She sat down on the one remaining chair at the table, which happened to be on his other side. "I'm saving my appetite for the barbecue chicken."

"It's all delicious. Especially this one, if I do say so myself." He gave a modest shrug.

"You're a pro." She smiled and he felt that connection between them tug a little harder.

"I love pizza. It's my favorite," Maya declared.

"Me too!" Alex said. "I could eat pizza every single day."

"It's my triple favorite," Jack, not to be outdone, announced. "I could eat it every day and every night."

Ava rolled her eyes. "You're such a dork."

The kids appeared to be done after finishing most of the second pizza.

"Can we go finish the show now?" Destry asked.

Caidy glanced at him. "As long as Dr. Caldwell doesn't mind sticking around a little longer."

He should leave. This kitchen—and the soft, beautiful woman in it—were just too appealing. A little fuel had helped push away some of the exhaustion, but he still worried his defenses were slipping around Caidy.

However, that barbecue chicken pizza currently baking was filling the kitchen with delicious, smoky smells. She had gone to all the effort to make it. He might as well stay to taste it.

"How much time is left on the show?" he asked.

"I don't know. Not that much, I'm sure," Destry said, rather artfully, he thought.

Caidy looked doubtful but she didn't argue with her niece.

"We can stay awhile more," he finally said. "If it goes on too much longer, we might have to leave before the show ends."

Despite the warning, his ruling was met with cheers from all the children.

"Thanks, Dad," Ava said, gifting him with one of her rare smiles. "We're having too much fun to go yet."

"I love this show," Jack said. "It's *hilarious*."

A new word in kindergarten apparently. He smiled, feeling rather heroic to give his children something they wanted. As soon as all the kids hurried out to start the show again, he realized his mistake. He was alone again with Caidy, surrounded by delicious smells and this dangerous connection shivering between them.

She rose quickly, ostensibly to check on the pizza, but he sensed she was also aware of it. As she slid the third pizza onto the peel and then out of the oven, he racked his brain to come up with a topic of polite conversation.

He could only come up with one. "What happened to your parents?"

The words came out more bluntly than he intended. Apparently, they startled her too. She nearly dropped the paddle, pizza and all, but recovered enough to carry it with both hands to the table, where she set it down between them.

"Wow. That was out of the blue."

He was an idiot who had no business being let out around anything with less than four feet. Or three, in Tri's case.

"It's none of my business. You don't have to tell me. I've been wondering, that's all. Sorry."

She sighed as she picked up the pizza slicer and jerked it across the pie. "What have you heard?"

"Nothing. Only what you've said, which isn't much. I've gathered it was something tragic. A car accident?"

She didn't answer for a moment, busy with slicing

the pizza and lifting a piece to a plate for him and then
for herself. He was very sorry he had said anything, especially when it obviously caused her so much sadness.

"It wasn't a car accident," she finally said. "Sometimes I wish it were something as straightforward as
that. It might have been easier."

He took a bite of his pizza. The robust flavors melted
on his tongue but he hardly noticed them as he waited
for her to continue.

She took a small bite of hers and then a sip of the
root beer before she spoke again. "It wasn't any kind of
accident," she said. "They were murdered."

He hadn't expected that one, not here in quiet Pine
Gulch. He stared at the tightness of her mouth that could
be so lush and delicious. "Murdered? Seriously?"

She nodded. "I know. It still doesn't seem real to me
either. It's been eleven years now and I don't know if
any of us has ever really gotten over it."

"You must have been just a girl."

"Sixteen." She spoke the word softly and he felt a
pang of regret for a girl who had lost her father and
mother at such a tender age.

"Was it someone they knew?"

"We don't know who killed them. That's one of the
toughest aspects of the whole thing. It's still unsolved.
We do know it was two men. One dark-haired, one
blond, in their late twenties."

Her mouth tightened more and she sipped at her root
beer. He wanted to kick himself for bringing up this obviously painful topic.

"They were both strangers to Pine Gulch," she went
on. "That much we know. But they didn't leave any fin-
gerprints or other clues. Only, uh, one shaky eyewit-
ness identification."

"What was the motive?"

"Oh, robbery. The whole thing was motivated by greed. My parents had an extensive art collection. I know you saw the painting in the dining room the other day and probably figured out our mother was a brilliant artist. She also had many close friends in the art community who gave her gifts of their work or sold them to her at a steep discount."

A brazen art theft here in quiet Pine Gulch. Of all the things he might have guessed, that was just about last on the list.

"It was a few days before Christmas. Eleven years ago tomorrow, actually. None of the boys lived at home then, only me. Ridge was working up in Montana, Trace was in the military and Taft had an apartment in town. No one was supposed to be here that night. I had a Christmas concert that night at the high school but I...I was ill. Or said I was anyway."

"You weren't?"

She set her fork down next to her mostly uneaten pizza and he felt guilty again for interrupting her meal with this tragic topic. He wanted to tell her not to finish, that he didn't need to know, but he was afraid that sounded even more stupid—and besides that, he sensed some part of her needed to tell him.

"It's so stupid. I was a stupid, selfish, silly sixteen-year-old girl. My boyfriend, Cody Spencer—the asshole—had just broken up with me that morning in homeroom. He wanted to go out with my best friend, if you can believe that cliché. And Sarah Beth had wanted him ever since we started going out and decided dating the captain of the football team and president of the performance choir was more important than friendship.

I was quite certain, as only a sixteen-year-old girl can be, that my heart had broken in a million little pieces."

He tried to picture her at sixteen and couldn't form a good picture. Was it because that pivotal event had changed her so drastically?

"The worst part was, Cody and I were supposed to sing a duet together at the choir concert—'Merry Christmas, Darling.' I couldn't go through with it. I just…couldn't. So I told my parents I thought I must have food poisoning. I don't think they believed me for a minute, but what else could they do when I told them I would throw up if I had to go onstage that night? They agreed to stay home with me. None of us knew it would be a fatal mistake."

"You couldn't have known."

"I know that intellectually, but it's still easy to blame myself."

"Easy, maybe, but not fair to a sixteen-year-old girl with a broken heart."

She gave him a surprised look, as if she hadn't expected him to demonstrate any sort of understanding. Did she think him as much an asshole as Cody Spencer?

"I know. It wasn't my fault. It just…feels that way sometimes. It happened right here, you know. In the kitchen. They disarmed the security system and broke in through the back door over there. My mom and I were in here when we heard them outside. I caught a quick glimpse of their faces through the window before my mother shoved me into the pantry and ordered me to stay put. I thought she was coming in after me so I hid under the bottom shelf to make room for her, but…she went back out again, calling for my father."

She was silent and he didn't know what to say, what to do, to ease the torment in her eyes. Finally, he settled for resting a hand over hers on the table. She gave him another of those surprised looks, then turned her hand over so they were palm against palm and twisted her fingers in his.

"The men ordered her to the ground and…I could hear them arguing. With her, with themselves. One wanted to leave but the other one said it was too late, she had seen them. And then my father came in. He must have had one of his hunting rifles trained on them. I couldn't see from inside the pantry, but the next thing I knew, two shots rang out. The police said my dad and one of the men must have fired at each other at the same moment. The other guy was hit and injured. My dad… died instantly."

"Oh, Caidy."

"After that, it was crazy. My mom was screaming at them. She grabbed a knife out of the kitchen and went after them and the…the bastard shot her too. She…took a while to die. I could hear her breathing while the men hurried through the house taking the art they wanted. They must have made about four or five trips outside before they finally left. And I stayed inside that pantry, doing nothing. I tried to help my mother once but she made me go back inside. I didn't know what else to do."

Outside the kitchen he could hear laughter from the children at something on the show they were watching. Caidy's fingers trembled slightly, her skin cool now, and he tightened his hand around hers.

"I should have helped her. Maybe I could have done something."

"You would have been shot if they'd known you were here."

"Maybe."

"No 'maybe' about it. Do you think they would have

hesitated for a moment?" He couldn't bear thinking about the horrific possibility.

"I don't know. I... When I finally heard them drive away, I waited several more minutes to make sure they weren't coming back, then went out to call nine-one-one. By then, it was too late for my mother. She was barely hanging on when Taft and the rest of the paramedics arrived. Maybe if I had called earlier, she wouldn't have lost so much blood."

Everything made so much sense now. The close bond between the siblings masked a deep pain. He had sensed it and now he knew the root of it.

Did that explain why she was still here at the River Bow all these years later, why she hadn't finished veterinary school? Did guilt keep her here, still figuratively hiding in the pantry?

Was this the reason she didn't sing anymore?

He curled her fingers in his, wishing he had some other way to ease her burden. "It wasn't your fault. What a horrible thing to happen to anyone, let alone a young girl."

"I guess you understand now why I don't like Christmas much. I try, for Destry's sake. She wasn't even born then. It doesn't seem fair to make her miss out on all the holiday fun because of grief for people she doesn't know."

"I can see that."

Much to his disappointment, she slid her hand out from underneath his and rose to take her plate to the sink. Though he sensed she was trying to create distance between them again, he cleared his own dishes and carried them to the sink after her.

She looked surprised. "Oh, thanks. You didn't have to do that. You're a guest."

"A guest who owes you far more the few moments it takes to bus a few dishes," he countered before returning to the table to clean up the mess of plates and napkins and glasses the children had left behind.

She smiled her thanks when he carried the things to the sink and he wanted to think some of the grimness had left her expression. She still hadn't eaten much pizza but he decided it wasn't his place to nag her about that.

He grabbed a dish towel and started to dry the few dishes in the drainer by the sink. Though she looked as if she wanted to argue, she said nothing and for a few moments they worked in companionable silence.

"My mom really loved the holidays," she said when the last few dishes were nearly finished. "Both of my parents did, really. I think that's what makes it harder. Mom would decorate the house even before Thanksgiving and she would spend the whole month baking. I think Dad was more excited than us kids. He used to sing Christmas songs at the top of his lungs. All through December—after we were done with chores and dinner and homework—he would gather us around the big grand piano in the other room to sing with him. Whatever musical talent I had came from him."

"I'd like to hear you sing," he said.

She gave him a sidelong look and shook her head. "I told you, I don't sing anymore."

"You think your parents would approve of that particular stance?"

She sighed and hung the dish towel on the handle of the big six-burner stove. "I know. I tell myself that every year. My dad, in particular, would be very disappointed in me. He would look at me underneath those bushy eyebrows of his and tell me music is the medicine of a broken heart. That was one of his favorite sayings. Or he would quote Nietzsche: 'without music, life is a mistake.' I know that intellectually, but sometimes what we know in our head doesn't always translate very well to our heart."

"Tell me about it," he muttered.

She gave him a curious look, leaning a hip against the work island.

He knew he should keep his mouth shut but somehow the words spilled out, like a song he didn't realize he knew. "My head is telling me it's a completely ridiculous idea to kiss you again."

She gazed at him for a long, silent moment, her eyes huge and her lips slightly parted. He saw her give a long, slow inhale. "And does your heart have other ideas? I hope so."

"The kids—" he said, rather ridiculously.

"—are busy watching a show and paying absolutely no mind to us in here," she finished.

He took a step forward, almost against his will. "This thing between us is crazy."

"Completely insane," she agreed.

"I don't know what's wrong with me."

"Probably the same thing that's wrong with me," she murmured, her voice husky and low. She also took a step forward, until she was only a breath away, until he was intoxicated by the scent of her, fresh and clean and lovely.

He had to kiss her. It seemed as inevitable as the sunrise over the mountains. He covered the space between them and brushed his mouth against hers once, twice, a third time. He might have found the willpower to stop there but she sighed his name and gripped the front of his shirt with both hands, leaning in for more, and he was lost.

She tasted of root beer—vanilla and mint. Delicious. He couldn't seem to get enough. He forgot everything when she was in his arms—his exhaustion, the music she didn't sing, the children in the other room.

All he could think about was Caidy, sweet and warm and lovely.

There was something intensely *right* about being here with her. He couldn't have explained it, other than he felt as if with every passing moment, some dark, empty corner inside him was being filled with soothing light.

She thought their first kiss that night at the clinic had been fantastic. This surpassed that one. The physical reaction was the same, instant heat and hunger, this wild surge of desire for more and more.

But she had barely known him that first time. Now she wasn't only kissing the very sexy veterinarian who had saved Luke's life. She was kissing the man who treated sweet Maya with such kindness, who looked adorably out of his depth making pizza but who trudged gamely on, who listened to her talk about her past without judgment or scorn but with compassion for the frightened young girl she had been.

She was kissing Ben, the man she was falling in love with.

She wrapped her arms around him, wanting to soak up every moment of the kiss. They kissed for several moments more, until his hand had slipped beneath the edge of her shirt to trace delicious patterns on her bare skin at her waist.

They might have continued kissing there in the

quiet kitchen for a long time but the children suddenly laughed hard at something in the other room and Ben stiffened as if someone had dropped snow down his back.

He slid his mouth away from hers. "We've got to stop doing this." His voice sounded ragged and his chest moved against her with each rapid breath.

"We...do?" She couldn't seem to make her brain work.

"Yes. This... I'm not being fair to you, Caidy."

Something in his tone finally penetrated the haze of desire around her and she took a deep breath and stepped away, willing herself to return to sensible thought.

"In what way?" She managed to make her voice sound cool and controlled, at odds with the tangled chaos of her thoughts.

He raked a hand through his hair, finishing the job of messing it that her own hands had started. "As much as I obviously...want you, I can't have a relationship right now. I'm not ready, the kids aren't ready. I've thrown too many changes at them in a very short time. A new town, a new school, a new job. Eventually a new house. I can't add another woman into the mix."

His words doused the last embers of heat between them. She shivered a little and pulled her shirt down while she struggled to chase after the tattered ends of her composure.

What could she say to that? He was right. His children had survived a great deal of tumult in a short time. The last thing she wanted to do was hurt Ava and Jack. They were great kids and she already cared for them. Just that afternoon, she felt as if she'd had a breakthrough with Ava when she had helped her ride around the practice ring on one of their more gentle horses.

Ben was the children's father. If he felt as though a relationship between him and Caidy would be harmful to his children, how could she argue?

He had obligations bigger than his own wants and needs. She had to accept that, no matter how painful.

Much to her horror, she could feel the heavy burn of tears. She never cried! She certainly couldn't remember ever crying over a *man*. Not since that idiot Cody Spencer when she was sixteen.

She took a deep breath and then another, concentrating hard on pushing the tears back. She didn't dare speak until she could trust her voice wouldn't wobble.

"I'm really glad we're on the same page here," she said, pretending a casual, breezy tone. "I'm not looking for a relationship right now. This attraction between us is…inconvenient, yes, but we're both adults. We can certainly ignore it for the short time you'll be living on the River Bow. After that, it shouldn't be a problem. I mean, how often do I need to take one of the dogs to the vet? We'll hardly ever see each other after you move into your new house."

Instead of reassuring him as to her insouciance, her words seemed to trouble him further. His brow furrowed and he gave her a searching look.

"Caidy—" he began, but Des came into the kitchen before he could complete the thought.

"You're still in here making pizza? This kitchen is so hot!"

Isn't that the truth? Caidy thought.

"You didn't even come in and watch the show with us and now it's almost over."

She seized on the diversion. "You really left the movie before the end?"

"Jack wanted more root beer. I told him I'd take care of it."

Ben made a face. "Jack has probably had all the root beer one kid needs for a night. How about we switch his beverage of choice to water? If he complains, you can tell him his mean old dad said no."

Destry grinned. "Right, Dr. Caldwell. Like anybody would believe you're mean. Or old."

"You'd be surprised," he muttered.

"Why don't you watch the end of the show with the kids?" she suggested.

"What about you?"

"I have a few things to take care of in here. After that, I'll be right in."

After a moment's hesitation, he nodded. "I can take Jack's water, if you'd like," he said to Destry, who handed over the cup and led the way to the television room.

When he was gone, taking all his heat and vitality and these seething emotions between them, Caidy slumped into a chair at the kitchen table and just barely refrained from burying her head in her hands.

She was becoming an idiot over Ben. All he needed to do was give her that rare, charming smile and her insides caught fire and she wanted to jump into his arms.

Worse than that, she was developing genuine feelings for him. How could she not? She remembered him at dinner with Maya and her heart seemed to melt.

She had to stop this or she would be in for serious heartbreak. He wasn't interested in a relationship. He had made that plain twice now. He didn't want anything she had to offer and she would be a fool if she allowed herself to forget that, even for a moment.

Okay, she could do this. A few more weeks and he would be gone from her life, for the most part. She would just have to work hard these remaining weeks while he was still on the River Bow to guard her emotions. Ben and his children could easily slip right past her defenses and into her heart. She was just going to have to do everything she could to keep that from happening, no matter how hard it might be.

Chapter Twelve

Three more days.

She could smile and make conversation and pretend to be excited about Christmas for three more days.

Less than three days actually. Two and a half, really. This was Sunday evening, the day before Christmas Eve. She had tonight, Christmas Eve and then Christmas Day to survive, and then she could toss another holiday into her personal history book.

Okay, that didn't count the week leading up to New Year's, but she wasn't going to think about that. Once Christmas itself was over, she usually could relax and enjoy the remaining days of the holidays and the time it gave her with her family.

For now, she had to survive this particular evening. Caidy stepped out of her bedroom wearing her best black slacks and a dressy white silk blouse she had worn only once before, to the annual cattleman's harvest dinner a few years earlier. With it, she wore a triple strand of colorful glass beads she had picked up at a craft fair that summer.

This was about as dressed up as she could manage. Was it too much? Not enough? She hated trying to figure out proper attire for parties, especially this one.

She fervently wished that she could stay home, pop a big batch of buttery popcorn and find something on TV that wasn't a sappy holiday special.

She had an excuse just about every year to avoid going to the big party Carson and Jenna McRaven had been hosting the past few years at Carson's huge house up Cold Creek Canyon, but Destry had begged and pleaded this year with both Ridge and Caidy.

Destry had trotted out a dozen reasons why they should make an exception and attend this year: all her friends were going. It was going to be *a blast*. Attending was the neighborly thing to do. The McRavens would think the Bowmans didn't like them if they continued to decline the invitation every year.

Finally, she pulled the "you just don't want me to have any fun" card and Ridge had reluctantly accepted his fate and agreed to go. Though she knew it was ridiculous, Caidy had felt obligated to accompany them both.

She wasn't looking forward to any aspect of the party except the food. Jenna was a fantastic cook and catered events all over the county. Her friend, though, tended to go a little overboard when it came to Christmas. Her very gorgeous husband did too. Raven's Nest was always decorated to the hilt for the holidays and the McRavens loved hosting holiday gatherings for family and friends.

She could get through it, she told herself. Less than seventy-two hours, right? With that little pep talk firmly in mind, she headed for the kitchen for the two Dutch apple pies she had baked that morning and found both Destry and Ridge there.

"Oh, you look beautiful, Aunt Caidy!" Destry exclaimed.

Ridge gave one of his rare smiles. "It's true, sis. You do. Much too fancy to be saddled with the likes of us."

Her oldest brother looked handsome and commanding, as usual, in a Western-cut shirt and one of his favorite bolo ties while Destry wore her best pair of jeans and the cute wintry sweater they had bought in Jackson the last time they went shopping together.

At the neckline, Caidy could see the flowered straps of her swimming suit peeking through.

"You're all set to swim?"

The McRavens had the only private indoor pool in town and it was a big hit among the area kids. The stuff of legend.

Destry lifted a mesh bag off the table. "I've got everything here. I can't wait. I've heard it's a superawesome pool. That's what Tallie and Claire told me. I just hope Kip Wheeler isn't too much of a tease. He can be *such* a pest."

Kip was Jenna's son from her first marriage, which had ended in the tragic death of her husband several years ago. He and his two older brothers and younger sister had been adopted by Carson McRaven after he married Jenna. They now had a busy toddler of their own, who kept all of them hopping.

"Everybody ready?"

"I am!" Destry jumped up and threw on her coat.

"As I'll ever be," Caidy muttered. Ridge gave her a sympathetic look as he lifted one of the pies and carried it out to the Suburban.

A light snow speckled the windshield, reflecting the

colorful holiday light displays they passed on their way to the McRavens' house. They approached the house through a long line of parked cars on either side of the curving driveway. It looked as if half the town was inside the big house. She recognized Trace's SUV and Taft's extended-cab pickup. Apparently, even when they canceled the regular Sunday night Bowman dinner for a special occasion, the family couldn't manage to stay apart.

"I'll let you two off near the door, then find a place to park," Ridge said.

She wanted to tell him to forget it, but because she was wearing her completely impractical high-heeled black boots, she didn't argue.

"Want me to take a pie inside?" Destry asked.

"You've got your swim stuff. I can manage," she answered.

As she expected, the entrance to the McRavens' house was beautifully decorated with grapevine garlands entwined with evergreens and twinkling lights. A trio of small live trees was also adorned with lights.

The door opened before they could even knock and Jenna McRaven answered. She smiled, pretty and blonde and deceptively fragile-looking. "Oh, Caidy. You made it! I thought the day would never come when we could convince you to come to our Christmas party."

Carson joined her at the door and gave all of them a wide, charming smile. He was vastly different from the cold man she remembered coming to town five years ago.

"Caidy, great to see you." He kissed Caidy's cheek before slipping an arm around his wife. The two of them plainly adored each other. Caidy had noticed before that when they were together, scarcely a moment passed when one of them didn't touch the other in some way. A hand on the arm, a brush of fingers.

She told herself she had no right to be envious of their happiness together.

"And you brought food!" Carson exclaimed.

"Where would you like the pies?"

"Besides in my stomach?" Carson asked. "They look fantastic. We can probably find room on the dessert table. What am I saying? There's always room for pie."

"I'll help you," Jenna said, taking one of the pies. "Carson, will you show Destry where she can change into her swimming suit?"

"I've already got it on," Des proclaimed, yanking the neck of her sweater aside to show the swimming suit strap.

"Good thinking." Carson smiled at her. "I'll just show you where you can leave your things, then."

They walked away and Jenna led her into the opposite direction, into the beautiful gourmet kitchen of the home, which currently bustled with about a dozen of her friends.

"Hey, Caidy!" Emery Cavazos greeted her with a smile, looking elegant and composed as always while she transferred something chocolate and rich-looking onto a tray.

"Hi, Em."

Nothing to worry about in here, she thought. She loved these women and got together with them often at various social functions. She could just pretend this was one of their regular parties.

"You know, Caidy would be perfect for that little matter we were discussing earlier," Maggie Dalton exclaimed.

"What matter?" she asked warily. With the Cold Creek women, one could never be too careful.

"We've all been admiring the new vet—a gorgeous widower with those two adorable kids," Jenna said. "We were trying to figure out someone we could subtly introduce him to."

"We've already met." And locked lips. More than once. She decided to keep that tidbit of information to herself. If she didn't, the whole town would join her brothers in trying to hook her up with Ben, who had made it quite plain they would never be matched.

Caroline Dalton—married to the oldest Dalton brother, Wade—tilted her head and gave Caidy a long, considering look. "You know, Mag, I think you're absolutely right. She's perfect for him."

"I...am?"

"Yes! You both love animals and you're wonderful with children."

"We need to figure out some way to get them together." Emery, the traitor, joined into the scheming.

Had she become such an object of pity that all the women in town felt they had to step in and take drastic action to practically arrange a marriage for her? It was a depressing thought, especially because Ben had made it clear he wasn't even interested in *kissing* her.

"Thank you, but that's not necessary," she said quickly, hoping to cut off this disastrous conniving at the pass. "As I said, Dr. Caldwell and I have met. He treated a dog of mine who was injured a few weeks ago. And in case you didn't know, he's currently living on the foreman's cottage at the River Bow."

"Oh, I hadn't heard he and the children moved out of the inn," exclaimed Jenny Boyer Dalton, principal of the elementary school. "I'm so happy they're not stay-ing there for Christmas. No offense, Laura."

"None taken," Caidy's sister-in-law said. "I agree."

"That was a brilliant idea," Caroline said. "See, you *are* perfect for him!"

She could see this whole situation quickly spiral-ing out of control, with everybody in town jumping on board to push her and Ben together. What a nightmare that would be. He would hate it, especially when he had clearly brushed her off two nights ago after that stunning kiss.

In desperation, she hurried to try a little damage con-trol. "I think you all need to give Ben a break and let him settle into Pine Gulch before you start picking out china patterns for him. The poor man hasn't even had the chance to move into his own house yet."

He would be going soon, though. The house he was building would be finished after the holidays and he and the children would be moving off the River Bow. The thought of not seeing those lights gleaming in the windows of the foreman's cottage—of not having the chance to listen to Jack's knock-knock jokes or being able to tease a reluctant smile from Ava—filled her with a poignant sense of loss.

The rest of winter stretched out ahead of her, long and empty. Not just the winter. The months and years to come, each day the same as the one before.

She would miss all of them dearly. How would she live in Pine Gulch knowing he was so close but out of her reach?

Maybe the time had come for her to take a different path. She could probably find a job somewhere outside Pine Gulch. Separating from her family would be painful but she wasn't sure which would hurt more—leaving or staying.

"Only friends, huh? That's too bad." Maggie Dalton gave a rueful sigh. "Don't you think if you tried, you could stir up a little interest in more? I mean, the man is *hot*."

Yes, she was fully aware of that—and was positive none of these women had known the magic of his kiss. The problem wasn't how attractive she found Ben Caldwell. He didn't feel the same way about her and she couldn't figure out a darn thing to do about it.

She wanted to cry, suddenly, right here in front of her dearest friends—each of whom had the great fortune to be married to a wonderful man who loved her deeply. They were all so happily married, they wanted everyone else to know the same joy. Caidy didn't know how to tell them the likelihood of that happening to her was pathetically slim.

Not that she wanted that. She was perfectly happy right now.

"You'd be surprised how often friendship can develop into more," Emery said. "Dr. Caldwell really does seem like a nice guy. We don't get all that many available men in Cold Creek besides the guys who come to snowmobile or fish. Maybe you should think about seeing if he wants to be more than friends."

Those tears burned harder behind her eyelids. Coming to this party was a phenomenally bad idea. If she'd had any idea she would face a gauntlet of matchmakers, she would have hidden in her room and locked the door.

"Don't, okay? Just…don't. Ben and I are friends. That's all. Not everyone is destined to live happily ever after like all of you are. Is it so hard to believe that maybe I like my life the way it is? Maybe Ben does too. Back off, okay?"

Her friends gaped at her and she could tell her vehemence had shocked them. She wasn't usually so firm, she realized. Now they were going to wonder why this was such a hot button for her.

Damn.

And Laura knew she and Ben had kissed. She was going to have to hope her beloved sister-in-law didn't decide to mention that little fact to the rest of the women.

She just couldn't win. Sometimes escaping with the remains of her dignity was the best option.

"I need to take one of my pies out to the dessert table. What about that tray, Emery? Is it ready to go out?"

"Um, sure." Her friend handed the delicious-looking bar cookies to her without another word. Feeling the heat of all their gazes on her back, Caidy escaped from the kitchen.

The party was crowded and noisy. For all its size, having a hundred people, many of them children, crammed into the McRavens' house didn't lend itself to quiet, relaxing conversation. Several neighbors and friends greeted her on her way to the food tables and she tried to smile and talk with them for a few moments but quickly broke away, using the excuse of the treats.

The tables were covered with all manner of culinary delights, as she had expected. Jenna loved to cook and loved coming up with new recipes for her clients and family. Caidy didn't have much appetite but she filled a small plate with a few possibilities—to have something to hold, more than anything.

"Those look good. Any idea what they are?"

At the deep voice at her elbow, she whirled and her heart stuttered. How had she missed Ben's approach?

Probably a combination of the crowd and her own distraction.

"I'm not sure. Jenna is famous for her spinach pinwheels, so that's what I'm hoping for. I should tell her to put signs up so we know what we're eating."

He smiled and she wanted to drink in the sight of him, tall and gorgeous and dearly familiar.

"I hadn't realized you were coming to the McRavens' party," she said rather inanely. As always, she felt as if she were operating on half-brain capacity around him. "It's a bit of a legend around here."

"Mrs. McRaven invited us when they brought their dog Frank in to me last week. Apparently he swallowed a Lego, but the trouble, uh, passed. I thought coming to the party might be a good way to get to know some of the neighbors."

He tilted his head and studied her and she could feel herself flush. She had to hope none of her friends decided to come out of the kitchen just now to see her standing flustered and off balance next to Ben Caldwell.

"What about you?" he said. "I didn't expect to see you here. It's kind of hard to escape the holiday spirit in a crowd like this."

Had he *wondered* if she would come? She wasn't sure she wanted to know.

"Destry begged and begged this year. All her cousins and most of her friends were coming."

Before he could respond, someone jostled her from behind. She wobbled a little in her impractical boots and would have fallen if he hadn't reached out and grabbed her. For a charged moment, they stared at each other and she saw heat and hunger leap into his eyes.

The noise of the crowd seemed to fade away as if someone had switched down the volume, and she was aware of nothing but Ben. Of his arms, strong and comforting, of his firm mouth that had tasted so delicious against hers, of his eyes that studied her with desire and something else, something glittery and bright she couldn't identify.

"Oh. I'm so sorry. Are you all right, my dear?"

She recognized Marjorie Montgomery's voice and realized the mayor's wife—and the Dalton boys' mother—must have been the one who bumped into her. Still breathless—and grateful she had just set her plate on the table before she was jostled, so at least she didn't have spinach pinwheel smeared all over both of them—she managed to extricate herself from Ben's arms and turned.

"I'm fine. No problem."

Marjorie smiled innocently at her but she thought she saw a crafty light in the older woman's eyes. Oh, great. She and Ben would have no peace now that her friends had decided they were destined for each other. She wondered if she ought to warn him but decided that would just be too awkward.

"It's crazy in here," Ben said. "I saw some open chairs over by the French doors into the pool if you're looking for a place to sit down."

She didn't miss the delight in Marjorie's eyes. The woman probably thought her transparent ploy was paying off. She ought to politely decline and keep as far away as she could from Ben. The last thing she wanted to do was give anybody else ideas about linking the two of them.

But she was weak when it came to him and she couldn't resist spending whatever time she had with him, even though he had made it quite clear they couldn't have a relationship. Maybe, like her, he knew he should stay away but couldn't quite manage it.

She probably shouldn't find that so heartening.

"Sure." She picked up her plate and a glass of water and headed with him toward the chairs he indicated.

"Where are the kids?"

"Where else? In the pool." He gestured through the glass doors and she saw Jack playing in the shallow end with Laura's son, Alex. Ava was huddled with a group of girls, including Destry and Gabi.

"Taft offered to keep an eye on them for me so I could grab something to eat, since he was watching Alex and Maya anyway. I figured they were pretty safe with the fire chief on lifeguard duty."

They lapsed into silence and she nibbled at a little delicacy that tasted of pumpkin and cinnamon.

"So are you ready for Christmas?" she finally asked when the silence grew awkward. She regretted the words the instant they left her mouth. Good grief, could she sound any more mindless?

"No. Not at all," he answered with a slight note of panic in his voice. "I should be home wrapping presents right now. I don't know the first thing about how to do that. My wife usually took care of those details and then Mrs. Michaels has stepped in since Brooke died. Maybe I'll tell the kids Santa decided not to wrap the presents this year and just jumble them under the tree."

"You can't do that! The mystery and anticipation of unwrapping the gifts is part of the magic!"

He raised an eyebrow. "Says the woman who would like to forget all about the holidays."

"Just because I don't particularly enjoy Christmas doesn't mean I don't know what makes the day a perfect one, especially for children," she protested. "Destry's gifts have been wrapped and hidden away since Thanksgiving."

He was quiet for a long moment and then he shook his head. "You're remarkable, aren't you?"

His words baffled her. Was he making fun of her? "Why do you say that?"

"You hate Christmas but wouldn't think for a moment of short-shrifting your niece in any way. I just find that amazing. You really love her, don't you?"

She watched Destry through the glass, now playing ball with the other girls. "I do. She's the daughter I'll probably never have."

"Why not? You're young. What makes you think you won't have a family of your own someday?"

She wanted to answer that she was very much afraid she was falling in love with a veterinarian who had made it plain he was only interested in friendship, but of course she couldn't. "Some of us are just meant to be favorite aunts, I guess."

Before he could respond to what she suddenly realized sounded rather pathetic, she quickly changed the subject. "Do you want some help with the children's presents? I can sneak over after they're in bed tonight and help you wrap them. How long would it take? An hour, maybe. Tops."

He stared at her for a long moment, then shook his head. "I'm sure that's not necessary. I'll probably fumble my way through. Or just leave things unwrapped. It won't be the end of the world."

Another rejection. She almost sighed. She should be used to it by now. This time she had only been offering to help him but apparently even that was more than he wanted from her.

"No problem. I wouldn't want to impose."

"That's my line. I don't want you to feel obligated to come over at midnight on a pity mission to wrap presents for the inept single father."

"I never even thought of it that way!" she exclaimed. "I only wanted to… I don't know. Ease your burden a little."

He opened his mouth and then closed it again, an odd light in his eyes. "In that case, all right," he said after a long moment. "Everything is so crazy this year, with the rented house and Mrs. Michaels gone. I probably should try to keep the rest of our holiday traditions as consistent as possible. Santa Claus has always wrapped their gifts. I'm sure Jack won't care but Ava will probably consider it another failing of mine if I don't do things the way she's used to."

He paused. "I'm afraid my ledger of debt to you is growing longer and longer."

She managed a smile. "Friends don't keep track of things like that, Ben."

Because that's all they apparently would ever be, at least she could be the best damn friend he'd ever had.

"Thank you."

She couldn't sit here and make polite conversation with him, she decided. Not when she wanted so much more.

"Oh, there's Becca and Trace. I promised Becca I would talk to her about the menu for Christmas dinner. I should go do that. Will you excuse me?"

He rose. "Sure."

"I'm serious about helping you with the presents. Why don't you call me after the kids are asleep and I'll run over?"

He looked rueful. "I should refuse. This is something

I should probably be able to handle myself, but the truth is I'm grateful for your help."

She smiled, doing her best to conceal any trace of yearning, and walked away from him.

She was twenty-seven years old and had just discovered she must have a streak of masochism. Why else would she continue to thrust herself into situations that would only bump up her heartache?

Chapter Thirteen

Ben gazed at his phone, at the OK. They're asleep text message he had typed but hadn't sent.

He should delete it right now and tell her he had changed his mind. Caidy Bowman was dangerous to him, especially at ten-thirty at night.

He thought of how beautiful she had looked at the McRavens' party, sweetly lovely, like a spun sugar Christmas angel. The first moment he saw her at the party, standing by the refreshment table, he had been stunned by his desire to whirl her around and into his arms. As ridiculously medieval as it sounded, he had wanted to kiss her soundly and claim her as his for everyone at the party to see.

"I'm crazy, Tri, aren't I?"

The chihuahua cocked his head and appeared to ponder the question.

"Never mind. It was rhetorical. You don't have to answer."

Tri yipped and jumped into his lap with amazing agility for a three-legged dog. Resilient, the little dog, adjusting to whatever challenges life delivered to him. Ben could only wish for a small portion of the dog's courage.

He glanced at his phone again and without taking time to think it through, he hit the send button before he could change his mind.

Her answer came instantly, as if she had been waiting for him: Be right there.

Something in his chest gave a silly little kick and he shook his head, reminding himself of all the very valid reasons he had given her a few nights earlier. He wasn't in a good place for a relationship with her. His kids were struggling enough with this move. He couldn't suddenly throw a woman into the chaos to distract his attention from their needs.

This would be the last time, he told himself. He would accept her help with his presents and then he had to do a better job of maintaining a safe distance from her. He had talked to his contractor at the party and learned the house was on schedule to be finished in about ten days, just after the New Year. Maybe when he moved a few miles away, he could regain a little perspective and be able to spend a few moments of the day without thinking about her, longing for her.

"Yeah, I'm crazy," he said to Tri. He set the dog onto the ground and headed for Mrs. Michaels's room, where all the children's presents were hidden in her locked closet.

Before she left, she had wrapped a few of the presents. He found plenty of wrapping paper, tape and scissors in the closet. *Efficient Anne,* he thought fondly, missing her calming presence in his life. If not for the chaos of living in a hotel and then moving here to the ranch, his housekeeper probably would have finished the job weeks ago.

He carried the wrapping supplies down to the table in the kitchen. After a careful look inside the children's room to make sure they were soundly sleeping, he made a few more quiet trips up and down the stairs to transport the unwrapped gifts to the table.

Just as he finished the last load, he saw a flicker of movement outside and then Caidy approaching from the ranch house, making her way through the lightly falling snow. She had a couple of dogs with her and carried two large reusable shopping bags that piqued his curiosity. As she neared the porch steps, she gestured with one of her hands and gave an order to the dogs. Though he couldn't hear what she said, he guessed she was telling them to go back home. One of the dogs moved with eagerness ahead of the other, which seemed to trudge behind more slowly.

Caidy watched the dog in the moonlight for a moment and when she turned, he thought she looked worried about something but he didn't have time to wonder about it before she climbed the steps and knocked softly on the door.

She was bundled up from head to toe in a heavy wool coat and nubby red scarf and hat. With her cheeks rosy from the cold, she looked delicious.

"Hi," she said, her voice pitched low, probably afraid of waking the children.

"Hello," he murmured and was struck by the quiet intimacy of the night. With the fire crackling in the living room and the snow falling softly, it would be easy to make the mistake of thinking they were alone here, tucked away against the world.

Tri greeted her with a few eager sniffs of her boots and she smiled at the dog. "Hi there. How are you, little friend?"

The dog seemed to grin at her and Ben wished for a little of that easy charm.

"What's all this?" he asked, gesturing to her shopping bags.

"Christmas dinner. My arms are going to fall off if I don't set it down. Can I put it in the kitchen?"

"Of course. What do you mean, Christmas dinner?"

"It's not much. We had an extra ham and I always keep mashed potatoes in the freezer. You just have to add a little milk when you reheat them in the microwave. And then I always make too much pie so I brought one of those too. Without Mrs. Michaels, I wasn't sure if you would have had much time to think about fixing something nice for you and the kids."

Right now he couldn't think much beyond the next meal he had to fix for the kids. Christmas dinner. She went to all that trouble?

Against his will, warmth seeped through him. Her thoughtfulness astounded him and he didn't quite know what to say.

"Thank you," he finally managed to say. "Wow. Just...thank you."

She smiled and the sweetness of it nearly took his breath away. "You're welcome. Shall I put it in the refrigerator?"

He stirred himself to reach for the bags. "That would be great."

Caidy Bowman astonished him. She had endured unimaginable horror and pain. Despite it, she was a nurturer, doing her best to make the world around her a little brighter.

For the next few moments, he pulled out package after package. It was more than just ham and potatoes. She had sent a jar of homemade strawberry jam, some frozen bread dough with instructions for thawing and baking written on them, even a small cheese ball and a box of crackers.

He was sure he would have muddled through some kind of dinner with the children, but the fact that she had thought far enough ahead to help touched something deep inside him.

I just want to help lift your burden a little, she had said earlier in the evening. He couldn't remember anybody ever spontaneously offering such a thing to him. Mrs. Michaels helped him tremendously but he paid her well for it. This was pure generosity on Caidy's part and he was stunned by it.

"Shall we get started with wrapping?"

He wasn't sure he trusted himself right now to spend five minutes with her, but because she had come all this way—and brought Christmas dinner to boot—he didn't know how to kick her out into the snow.

"I've brought everything down, including all the wrapping paper I could find."

"Perfect."

She took in the pile of presents with a slight smile dancing across that expressive mouth. "Looks like the children will have a great Christmas."

He hurried to disabuse her of the notion that he ought to win any Father of the Year awards. "Mrs. Michaels did a lot of the shopping, though I did buy a few things online. So where do we start?"

"I guess we just dive in. You know, I can handle this, if you have something else to do."

Did she want him to leave? For an instant, he was unbelievably tempted to do just that, escape into another room and leave her to it. But not only would that be rude, it would be cowardly too, especially when she had gone to all this trouble to walk down in the snow—and carrying a sumptuous meal too.

"No. Let's do this. With both of us working together, it shouldn't take long. You might have to babysit me a little."

"Surely you've wrapped a present before."

He racked his brain and vaguely remembered wrapping a gift for his grandparents that first Christmas after they had taken him in, a macaroni-covered pencil holder he had worked hard on in school. His grandfather hadn't even opened it, had made some excuse about saving it for later. Christmas night when he had taken out a bag of discarded wrapping paper, he had seen it out in the trash can, still wrapped.

"I probably did when I was a kid. I doubt my skills have improved since then."

"How can a man reach thirtysomething without learning how to wrap a present?"

"I rely on two really cool inventions. You may have heard of them. Store gift-wrapping and the very handy and ubiquitous gift bag."

She laughed, and the sound of it in the quiet kitchen entranced him. "I'll tell you what. I'll take care of all the oddly shaped gifts and you can handle the easy things. The books and the DVDs and other basic shapes. It's a piece of cake. Let me show you."

For the next few moments, he endured the sheer torture of having her stand at his side, her soft curves just a breath away as she leaned over the table beside him.

"The real trick to a beautifully wrapped present is to make sure you measure the paper correctly. Too big and you've got unsightly extra paper to deal with. Too small and the package underneath shows through."

"Makes sense," he mumbled. He was almost painfully aware of her, but beneath his desire was something deeper, a tenderness that terrified him. He meant his words to her earlier in the evening. She was an amazing person and he didn't know how much longer he could continue to ignore this inexorable bond between them.

"Okay, after you've measured your paper, leaving an extra inch or two on all sides, you bring the sides up, one over the other, and tape the seam. Great. Now fold the top and bottom edges of the end on the diagonal like this—" she demonstrated "—and then tape those down. Small pieces of tape are better. Can you see that?"

Right now, he would agree to anything she said. She smelled delicious and he wanted to pull her onto his lap and just nuzzle her neck for a few hours. "Okay. Sure."

"After that, you can use ribbon to wrap around it or just stick on a bow. Doesn't it look great? Do you think you can do it now on your own?"

He looked down blankly at the present. "Not really," he admitted.

She frowned, so close to him he could see the shimmery gold flecks in her eyes. "What part didn't you get? I thought that was a great demonstration."

He sighed. "It probably was. I only heard about half of it. I was too busy remembering how your mouth tastes like strawberries."

She stared at him for a long charged moment and

then she quickly moved to the chair across the table from him.

"Please stop," she said, her voice low and her color high.

"I'd like to. Believe me."

"I'm serious. I can't handle this back-and-forth thing. It's not fair. You flirt with me one minute and then push me away the next. Please. Make up your mind, for heaven's sake. I don't know what you want from me."

"I don't either," he admitted. He was an ass. She was absolutely right. "I think that's the problem. I keep telling myself I can't handle anything but friendship right now. Then you show up and you smell delicious and you're so sweet to bring dinner for us. To top it all off, you're so damned beautiful, all I can think about is kissing you again, holding you in my arms."

She stared at him, her eyes wide. He saw awareness there and something else, something fragile.

He wanted her fiercely. Because she trembled whenever he touched her, he suspected she shared his hunger. He could kiss her—and possibly do more—now, but at what cost?

She was a vulnerable woman. He was no armchair psychologist, but he guessed she was hiding herself away here on this ranch because she saw only weakness and fear in herself. She saw the sixteen-year-old girl who had cowered from her parents' killers. She didn't see herself as the strong, powerful, desirable woman he did.

He could hurt her—and that was the last thing he wanted to do.

"Sorry. Forget I said that. We'd better get these presents wrapped so you can go home and get some sleep."

She stared at him, her eyes wide and impossibly

green. Finally she nodded. "Yes. I would hate to be down here wrapping gifts if one of the children woke up and came down for a drink of water or something."

She turned her attention to the task at hand. He fumbled through wrapping a book for Ava and did an okay job but nothing as polished as Caidy's presents. After a few more awkward moments with only the sound of rustling paper and ripping tape, he decided he needed something as a buffer between them.

He rose from the table and headed for Mrs. Michaels's radio/CD player in the corner. When he turned it on, jazzy Christmas music filled the empty spaces. She didn't like holiday songs, he remembered, but she didn't seem to object so he left the station tuned there.

The pile dwindled between them, and at some point she started talking to him again, asking little questions about the gifts he and Mrs. Michaels had purchased, about the children's interests, about their early Christmases.

When he left to look for one more roll of paper in Mrs. Michaels's room, he returned to find her humming softly under her breath to "Angels We Have Heard on High," her voice soft and melodious.

He stood just on the other side of the doorway, wondering what it might take for her to sing again. She stopped abruptly when she sensed his presence and returned to taping up a box containing yet another outfit for Ava's American Girl doll.

"You found more paper. Oh, good. That should help us finish up."

He sat back down and started wrapping a DVD for Jack.

"Tell me about Christmas when you were a kid," she said after a moment.

That question came out of left field and he fumbled for an answer. "Fine. Nothing memorable."

"Everybody has some fond memory of Christmas. Making Christmas cookies, delivering gifts to neighbors. What were your traditions?"

He tried to think back and couldn't come up with much. "We usually had a nice tree. My grandmother's decorator would spend the whole day on it. It was really beautiful." He didn't add that he and Susie weren't allowed to go near it because of the thousands of dollars in glass ornaments adorning the branches.

"Your grandmother?"

Had he said that? "Yeah. My grandparents raised my sister and me from the time I was about eight until I left for college."

"Why?"

He could feel her gaze on him as he tried to come up with the words to answer her. He wanted to ignore it but couldn't figure out a way to do that politely. And suddenly, for a reason he couldn't have explained, he wanted to tell her, just like in his office earlier in the week when he had told her about Brooke.

"My childhood wasn't very happy, I guess, but I feel stupid complaining about it. I don't know who my father is. My mother was a drug addict who dumped my half sister and me on her parents and disappeared without a word. She died of an overdose about three months later."

Her eyes darkened with sympathy. "Oh, no. I'm so sorry. What a blessing that you had your grandparents to help you through it."

He gave a rough laugh. "My grandparents were extremely wealthy and important people in Chicago social circles but they didn't want to be saddled with the obligation of raising the children of an out-of-control daughter they had cut off years earlier. They probably would have chucked us into the foster care system if they weren't afraid of how it would look to their acquaintances. Sometimes I wish they had done just that. They didn't have the patience for two small children."

"Then it's even more wonderful that you work so hard to give your children such a great Christmas," she said promptly. "You've become the father you never had."

Her faith in him was humbling. At her words, he felt this shifting and settling inside his heart.

This wasn't simply attraction. He was in love with her. The realization settled over him like autumn leaves falling to earth, like that snow drifting against the windows.

How had *that* happened?

Perhaps during that sleigh ride, when he had seen her holding her sweet niece Maya on her lap, or when she had come to the door the other night, flour on her cheek from making three pizzas for a houseful of children. Or maybe that first night at the clinic, when she had knelt beside her injured dog and hummed away the animal's anxiety.

Oblivious to his sudden staggering epiphany, she tied an elaborate bow on the gift she was wrapping and snipped the ends. "There. That should be the last one."

Through his dazed shock, he managed to turn his attention to the pile of presents. Somehow he, Mrs. Michaels and Caidy had managed to pull off another Christmas.

She was right. He was a good father—not because he could provide them a pile of gifts but because he loved them, because he was doing his best to provide a safe, friendly place for them to grow, because he treated them with patience and respect instead of cold tolerance.

"Thank you." The words seemed inadequate for all she had done for him this holiday season.

She smiled and rose from the kitchen table. She stretched her arms over her head to work all the kinks out from being huddled over a table for nearly an hour, and it took all his strength not to leap across the table and devour her.

"Just imagining their faces on Christmas morning is enough thanks for me. You've got a couple of really adorable kids there, Ben."

"I do." His voice sounded strangled and she gave him an odd look but shrugged into her coat. He knew he should help her, but right now he didn't trust himself to be that close to her.

"Good night."

As she started for the door, he came to his senses. "I forgot you walked down here. Let me grab my coat and I'll walk you back to your house."

"That's not necessary."

It was to him. In answer, he pulled his coat down from the hook and drew it on while she watched him with a disgruntled expression.

"I've been walking this lane my whole life. I'm fine. You shouldn't leave the children."

"I'll be gone five minutes, with the house in view the whole time."

She sighed. "You're a stubborn man, Dr. Caldwell."

He could be. He supposed it was stubbornness that had kept him from admitting the truth to himself—that he was falling for her. As they walked out into the light snow, Tri hopping along ahead of them, he was struck again by the peace that seemed to enfold him when he was with her.

She smiled at the little dog's valiant efforts to stay in front as leader of the pack, then lifted her face to let snowflakes kiss her cheeks. Tenderness, sweet and healing, seemed to wash through him. He wanted to protect her, to make her smile—to, as she had said earlier, lift her burdens if she would let him.

His marriage hadn't quite been that way. He had loved Brooke but as he walked beside Caidy, he couldn't help thinking that in many ways it had been an immature sort of love. They had met when he had been in veterinary school and she had been doing undergraduate work in public relations.

For some reason he still didn't quite comprehend, she had immediately decided she wanted him, in that determined way she had, and he hadn't done much to change the course she set out for both of them.

He had come to love her, of course, though his love had been intertwined with gratitude that she would take a lonely, solitary man and give him a family and a place to belong.

He thought he would never fall in love again. When Brooke died, he thought his world was over. It had taken all these months and years for him to feel as though he could even think about moving forward with his life.

Here he was, though, crazy in love with Caidy Bowman and it scared the hell out of him. Could he risk his heart, his soul, all over again?

And why was he even thinking about this? Yes, Caidy responded to his kisses, but she had spent her adult life pushing away any relationship beyond her family. She might not even be interested in anything more with him. Why would she be? He didn't have that much to offer in the relationship department. He was surly and impatient, with a couple of energetic kids to boot.

"I wonder if I can ask you a favor," she said after they were nearly to the barn. "If you have time this week, could you take a look at my Sadie? I'm worried about her. She's not been acting like herself."

He pictured her old border collie, thirteen years old and moving with slow, measured movements. "Sure. I can come over tomorrow morning."

"Oh, I don't think it's urgent. After Christmas would probably be fine."

"All right. First thing Wednesday. Or if the kids and I feel like taking a walk after they open presents, maybe I'll stop up at the house to take a look."

"Thank you. You should probably go back. You left a fire in the fireplace, don't forget."

"Yes." He wanted to kiss her, here in the wintry cold. He wanted to tuck her against him and hold her close and keep her safe from any more sorrow.

He didn't have that right, he reminded himself. Not now. Maybe after the holidays, after he and the children moved into the new house and Mrs. Michaels came back, he could ask her to dinner, see where things might progress.

"Thank you again for your help with the gifts."

"You're welcome. If I don't see you again, merry Christmas."

"Same to you."

She gave that half smile again. Against his better judgment, he stepped forward and brushed a soft kiss on her rosy cheek, then turned around, scooped up his little dog and walked swiftly away through the snow—while he still could.

Chapter Fourteen

"Hang on. Just a few more moments. There's my sweet girl. Hang on."

Icy fear pulsed through Caidy as she drove her truck through the wintry Christmas Eve in a grim repeat of a scene she had already played a few weeks earlier with Luke. She was much more terrified this time than she had been with the younger dog, and the quarter mile to the foreman's cottage seemed to stretch on forever.

Sadie couldn't die. She just couldn't. But from the instant she had walked into the barn just moments earlier and found her beloved dog lying motionless in the straw of one of the stalls, all her vague concerns about the dog's health over the past few days had coalesced into this harsh, grinding terror.

Sadie, her dearest friend, was fading. She knew it in her heart and almost couldn't breathe around the pain.

She couldn't seem to think straight either. Only one thought managed to pierce her panic.

Ben would know what to do.

She had picked up the dog, shoved her into the bed of the nearest vehicle, Ridge's pickup, pulled the spare key out of the tackroom and drove like hell to Ben's place.

Now that she approached the house nestled in the pines, reality returned. It was nearly midnight on Christmas Eve. The children would be sound asleep. She couldn't rush in banging on the door to wake them up, tonight of all nights, when they would never be able to go back to sleep.

Adrenaline still shooting through her, she pulled up to the front door, trying to figure out what to do. The Christmas tree lights still blazed through the window. Maybe Ben was still awake.

Sadie hadn't made a sound this entire short trip, though Caidy could see her ribs still moving with her shallow breathing.

Caidy opened her door and was just trying to figure out which bedroom was his, wondering if she could throw a snowball at it or something in an effort to wake only him, when the porch light flicked on and the front door opened. An instant later, he walked out in stocking feet, squinting into the night.

"Caidy!" he exclaimed when he recognized her. "What is it? What's wrong?"

Relief poured through her, blessed relief. Ben would know what to do.

"It's Sadie," she said on a sob, hurrying to the passenger side of the pickup. "She's… Oh, please, Ben. Help me."

He didn't even stop to throw on shoes—he just raced

down the frozen sidewalk toward her. "Tell me what happened."

"I don't know. I just… After Destry and Ridge went to bed, I was just sitting by the Christmas tree by myself and I…I decided to go out to the barn. It's a…sacred sort of place on Christmas Eve, among the animals. Peaceful. I needed that tonight. But when I got there, I found Sadie lying in the straw. She wouldn't wake up."

She choked back her sob, knowing she needed to retain control if she had any hope of helping her beloved dog.

"Let's get her inside out of the cold and into the light so I can have a look at her."

He scooped the old dog into his arms and carried her back across that snowy walk. Caidy followed. Her heart felt as fragile as her mother's antique Christmas angel. How would she bear it if Sadie died tonight, of all nights?

No. She wasn't going to think about that. Only positive thoughts. Ben would take care of things, she was sure of it.

She thought of that day when she had taken Luke to the clinic, battered and broken. She had thought Ben so cold and uncaring. As she watched him gently lay Sadie on a blanket she had quickly grabbed from the sofa to spread in front of the still-glowing fireplace, she wondered if she had ever so poorly judged a person.

He was kind and compassionate. Wonderful. How could she ever have imagined that first day that he would become so dear to her?

"What's going on, girl?"

At least Sadie opened her eyes at his voice, but she didn't move as the veterinarian's hands moved over her, seeking answers.

"You said she hasn't been acting like herself. What have you seen?" he asked her.

She tried to think back over the past few days. The truth was, she had been so busy coping with the stress of Christmas, she hadn't paid as much attention to her dog as usual.

"She's been lethargic for three or four days. And it seems like on the nights when she wanted to sleep inside, she was always having to go out to pee. She hasn't eaten much, but she has been more thirsty than usual."

He frowned. "Exactly what I suspected."

"What?"

He looked at her with such gentleness, she wanted to weep. "I'll have to do labwork to be sure but I suspect she's having chronic kidney failure. It's not unusual in older dogs."

She drew in a heavy breath. "Can you…can you fix it?"

"The good news is, I can probably help her feel better tonight. She needs fluids and I always keep a few liters in my emergency kit. I can give her an IV right here."

"The bad news?"

"It's called chronic kidney failure for a reason," he said, his eyes compassionate. "There's no miracle cure, I'm afraid. We can perhaps make her more comfortable for a few months, but that's the best we can do. I'm so sorry, Caidy."

She nodded, those tears threatening again. "She's thirteen. I've known it was only a matter of time. But… even a few more months with her would be the greatest gift you could ever give me."

"I don't know for sure it's kidney failure. It could be something entirely different, but from the symptoms you describe and the exam, I'm ninety-nine percent certain. If you want me to, I can wait to treat her until I run bloodwork."

"No. I trust you. Completely." She paused. "I knew you would be able to help her. When I found her in the barn, all I could think about was bringing her to you."

He appeared startled at that, then gave her an unreadable look. "I'll go grab the supplies for an IV, then."

After he left the room, she knelt down beside the sweet-natured border collie, who had provided her with uncomplicated love and incalculable solace during the darkest moments of her life, when she had been a lost and grieving sixteen-year-old girl.

"Ben will help you," she told the dog, stroking her head softly. "You'll feel better soon. We can't have you missing your Christmas stocking. Here's a secret. Don't tell any of the others but I got you a new can of tennis balls. Your favorite."

Sadie's tail flapped halfheartedly on the carpet. It was a small sign of enthusiasm, yes, but more than Caidy had seen from the dog since she walked into the barn.

What would have happened if she hadn't found Sadie in time? The dog would never have made it. She was certain of that. When she and Destry and Ridge went out for chores on Christmas morning, they would have discovered her cold, lifeless body.

Just the thought of it made her stomach clutch. She *had* found her, though. Something had prompted her to brave the weather so she could find the dog in time and bring her here, to Ben, who knew just what to do.

Why *had* she gone out to the barn? Yes, she had found peace and solitude in the barn a few times before on Christmas Eve over the years, but it wasn't as if she made a habit of it.

She had been standing at the window gazing out at the cottage lights flickering in the trees, ready to collapse in her bed after a long day with her family, when some impulse she still didn't understand had compelled her to slip into her coat and head outside.

Coincidence? Maybe. Somehow she didn't think so. More like inspiration. Perhaps her own little miracle.

The thought raised chills on her arms as she gazed down at her beloved dog. What else could she call it? She had gone to the barn just in time to save a life. Even more miraculous, a wonderful veterinarian who knew just what to do lived just a quarter mile away—and he had the ready supplies necessary to help her dog.

Yes. A miracle.

A sweet sense of peace and love trickled over her, healing and cleansing, washing away the fear and sadness that had become so much a part of Christmas for her.

The clock on the mantel chimed softly. Midnight. It was Christmas. What better time for miracles, for second chances, for hope and light and life?

She leaned down to Sadie and began to hum one of her favorite Christmas songs, "It Came Upon a Midnight Clear." After a few bars, the words seemed to crowd through her heart, bursting to break free.

And for the first time in eleven years, she began to sing.

With the IV bag in his hand, Ben stood outside the room, afraid to move, to breathe, as he listened to the soft strains filling the air. He needed to help her dog quickly but surely he could wait a few more seconds.

Caidy was singing to her dog and her voice was the

most beautiful sound he had ever heard, clear and pure and sweet.

"The world in solemn stillness lay, to hear the angels sings."

As she finished the song, he forced himself to move into the room and knelt beside her and the dog. She glanced over, color soaking her cheeks.

"You don't have to stop," he said as he pulled on surgical gloves and went to work finding a spot for the IV. "In fact, I hope you don't. It appeared to comfort her."

She was silent for a moment and then she began to sing "Away in a Manger" in her sweet, lovely soprano. The song seemed to shimmer through the air.

"Your brother is right," he said when she sang the last note of the third verse. "You do have a beautiful voice. I feel blessed I had the chance to hear it."

She smiled a little tremulously. "I can't tell you how strange it feels to sing. Strange and wonderful. All this time, the music has been there, just waiting for me to let it out."

"I didn't know them but I can only imagine your parents would be happy you found your voice again." He knew he was taking a chance reminding her of the sadness that had become so much a part of her holidays.

To his relief, she nodded. "You're right. I know you're right."

Moving forward took tremendous courage. He was consumed with love for her and wanted to tell her so but the moment didn't seem right, when her beloved dog was struggling for life.

"Is there anything I can do right now for Sadie?"

He turned his full attention back to her dog. "I'm giving her a bolus now—a great deal of fluid in a short amount of time—and then we'll slowly drip the other bag over the next hour or so. I've also given her some medication in the IV that will help perk her up. We should see results fairly quickly. I'm afraid I'll have to keep her here for the night. Do you mind?"

"Mind?" She gave a rough laugh. "I don't know what I would have done without you, Ben."

"I guess it was my turn to ease your burden a little for a change."

Though she smiled, the Christmas lights from the tree she had given them reflected in green eyes that swam with tears. One dripped free and slid down her cheek and Ben reached his thumb out and brushed it away from her warm, silky skin. "Please don't cry."

"They're happy tears," she promised him. "Well, maybe a little bittersweet. I know she won't be here forever. But she's here now because of you. That's what matters—she's here. I don't think I could be strong enough to endure losing her on Christmas Eve."

"It's not Christmas Eve anymore. It's past midnight. Merry Christmas."

Her smile took his breath away and she leaned slightly into his hand. "Merry Christmas, Ben."

He caressed her cheek with his thumb, tenderness and love pulsing through him. Unable to resist, he framed her face with his hands and kissed her gently. She sighed softly and her arms slid around him.

The moment was so perfect there in his borrowed living room with the Christmas tree as a backdrop and he didn't want to do anything to break the spell, but he knew she couldn't be comfortable for long on her knees like that. He eased them both back against the armchair and sat there on the floor, pulling her almost onto his lap.

They kissed for a long moment with aching softness

and it was more magical than any Christmas morning he had dreamed about when he was a lonely boy. Love poured through him as sweetly as the notes of her song.

He loved this strong, courageous woman and needed her in his life. Jack and Ava did too. All his carefully constructed reasons for taking his time, moving slowly, seemed to fade into insignificance.

Yes, this might present another huge change for all of them, but he knew his children were resilient. They both liked Caidy already. Even Ava had said as much after the pizza night. It wouldn't take long for them to love her.

Finally she slid away, her eyes glimmering. She opened her mouth to speak and then must have decided she didn't want to disturb the peace of the moment. She turned slightly in his arms to check on Sadie. He held her as they both listened to the steady pump of the IV and watched the colored lights of the tree reflected in the window and plump snowflakes begin to fall.

After a few moments, Tri hopped in, probably emerging from his favorite sleeping spot at the foot of Ben's bed to wonder where he was. The little dog wandered over to Sadie, who was lying in front of the fire. Ben was about to call him off but Sadie's tail began to wag and she stirred herself to sniff at the other dog. Tri licked at her muzzle and then settled in next to her.

"Look at her." Caidy's laugh was filled with wonder.

"The medication metastasizes in her system fairly quickly. I imagine by the time the kids wake up, she'll have as much energy as they do."

"It's amazing. *You're* amazing."

When she looked at him that way, he felt like the most brilliant veterinarian in the country. She kissed him and though he knew some part of it was motivated by gratitude, he sensed something else in the way her mouth moved across his, the way her arms tightened around his neck.

Finally he knew he couldn't remain quiet any longer. "Do you think it's any kind of conflict of interest for a veterinarian to be in love with his patient's human?"

Caidy stared at him, certain the stress of the past half hour—coupled with her abject relief—must be playing tricks with her hearing. Did he just say...?

Her heart pounded as if that belligerent bull that had started this whole thing had just caught her in his sights and she couldn't seem to catch hold of any coherent thought. "Is that a hypothetical question?" she finally said, her voice low and thready.

Ben—wonderful, strong, brilliant Ben—tightened his arms around her, a soft, tender light in his eyes that made her catch her breath.

"I think you know the answer to that. I've been fighting this like crazy for a hundred different, stupid reasons. But tonight when I listened to you sing, I realized none of them matter. I love you, Caidy. I wasn't looking for it. Especially not now, when my life has so much chaos in it. I told myself I didn't want to take that kind of risk again."

He smiled at her and she felt as bright and sparkly as that angel on the top of the tree. "But here's the thing. Somehow, you calm the chaos. I don't know how you did it, but you burst into my life with your fierce courage and your dogs and your smile and turned everything I thought I wanted spinning into an entirely different direction."

"Ben," she said softly, unbelievably touched that the

man she thought so taciturn and hard that first day could be saying these words to her.

"I think I started to fall in love with you that day you came to the clinic, so determined to get the very best care for your dog. I knew for sure when you came here to help me wrap the children's presents the other night, even though you don't like Christmas."

"I don't know. I think my perspective on that is changing a little."

He laughed and kissed her again. When she slid away a few moments later, Sadie was sitting up, gazing around the room alertly while Tri teased at her ear. Caidy didn't know how her heart could contain more joy.

"To answer your question," she said, "I don't believe there is a conflict of interest at all as long as said veterinarian doesn't mind that the human in question is also very much in love with him."

"Is she?"

"Oh, yes. I love you. More than I can say. And Ava and Jack too. I thought I was content with my life here on the ranch helping Ridge, but over the past few weeks, I've come to realize something good and right has been missing. You. All this time, I think I've just been waiting for you."

He gazed at her for a long moment, his eyes fiery and bright, then with aching softness he picked up her hand and kissed her palm. "I'm here now. And I'm not going anywhere."

She couldn't contain the joy bubbling through her. Sadie would be all right, at least for now. It was Christmas morning, the time for miracles and hope, and she had eleven years of Christmases to make up for. What better place to do it than in the arms of the man she loved fiercely?

She wrapped her arms around him and Ben laughed softly, almost as if he couldn't help himself, then kissed her again while the Christmas tree lights gleamed and the two dogs snuggled by the fire and her heart sang.

Epilogue

"I just love Christmas weddings," Laura exclaimed as she adjusted one of the pins keeping Caidy's snowy-white veil in place.

"It's not Christmas," Maya said, with irrefutable logic. In the mirror, Caidy had a clear view of the little girl sitting on a bench in the room reserved for brides at the small church in Pine Gulch, carefully holding Trace and Becca's chubby six-month-old son, who was gumming his fingers.

"Santa doesn't come for five more days," Maya pointed out.

"True," her mother answered with a grin. "I should have said I love Christmas*time* weddings. Is that better?"

"Yes." Maya smiled, looking sweet and adorable in her blue-and-silver flower-girl dress.

"The church looks beautiful," Becca said, hurry-

ing in to scoop little Will out of Maya's lap with un-
erring instincts, just as both of the children started to
get bored with the arrangement. "It looks like a snowy
wonderland with all those silvery snowflakes and the
blue ribbons. Such a better choice than the traditional
red and green. As lovely as it is out there, it doesn't hold
a candle to our blushing bride here. You look fantastic.
Are you happy, Caidy?"

She smiled at her brothers' wives. She did feel a
small pang that her mother wasn't there on her wedding
day, but this was a time for joy, not sadness. She might
not have her mother with her, and that would always
hurt, but she did have these wonderful women who had
become so dear to her.

"*Happy* doesn't come close to covering it. I don't
think I have room inside me to hold all the joy."

"I don't either," Ava said, looking lovely in the
bridesmaid dress she was so very enthralled to be wearing.

"Same here," Destry, in a matching dress, added.

Caidy smiled and squeezed both girls' hands, the
daughter of her heart and the daughter she would be
gaining officially in a matter of moments.

Sometimes she couldn't take in the changes in her
life from last Christmas. Over the years, she had told
herself she was happy living at the ranch, helping her
brother with Destry, raising her dogs and her horses.
Now she could see how much power she had given one
horrible, violent event over her life. She had been hiding out there, slowly suffocating in her fears, afraid to
take any chances.

Ben had changed that. This past year had been filled
with more happiness than she could ever have imagined.
A little sadness too, she had to admit. After her miracu-

lous Christmas recovery, Sadie had made it to spring-time. Her last months she had shown more energy than she had in years, but one April morning Caidy had found her under the flowering branches of the crab-apple tree beside the house. Ben had helped her bury her friend on a hillside overlooking the ranch and the river and had held her while she wept.

The two of them had taken their time this past year, moving slowly to give the children time to adjust to the idea of her being a regular part of their lives.

Jack, with his sunny nature, had no problem accepting her. As she might have expected, Ava had been a little more resistant. At first, the girl had fought the idea of anyone wanting to replace her mother in their lives. But now, a year after she and Ben started dating, Caidy believed she and Ava had developed a strong, solid relationship.

A December wedding had been his idea, to give her something joyful to remember—instead of pain and fear—during this time of hope and promise.

Waiting all this time to start their lives together had seemed endless. The day was finally here and she couldn't imagine anything more perfect.

"I think you're ready now," Laura said. "Oh, Caidy. I'm so happy for you."

Taft's wife hugged her, though at four months pregnant, she was beginning to bump out a little.

"Same here," Becca said, kissing her cheek and squeezing her hands. "You deserve a wonderful guy like Ben. I'm really glad he turned out not to be a rude, arrogant, opinionated jerk."

Caidy cringed, remembering her stupid words about him so long ago. "None of you will let me forget that, will you?"

"Probably not." Laura smiled.

A knock sounded on the door. When Ava opened it, Ridge poked his head in, looking big and tough and gorgeous in his black Western-cut tuxedo. "Are we ready in here? I know a certain veterinarian who's a little impatient out there."

She drew a breath and adjusted her dress. "I think so."

"Come on, girls. Time to get in your places," Becca said.

Laura gave Caidy's veil one more adjustment, then stood back. "Okay. Perfect."

With a deep breath, Caidy slipped her hand in the crook of her brother's arm.

Ridge reached his other hand over and squeezed her fingers. "You're stunning," he said. "Mom and Dad would have been so proud of the beautiful woman you've become. Inside and out."

"Don't make me cry," she said, her throat thick with emotion.

"It's true. They would have liked Ben too. He's a good man. The highest praise I can give him is that I think he's almost good enough for you. I'm so glad you're happy."

She gave her brother a tremulous smile. "I am. It took me a while to get here but I really am."

"Let's do this, then."

The small but earnest church choir she now joined on Sundays broke into singing Pachelbel's "Canon in D Major" and she drew a deep breath, nerves skittering through her. As she and Ridge started down the aisle behind the bridesmaids, she looked down and saw the gruff, sometimes taciturn veterinarian she loved be-

yond measure smiling broadly. The best man—Jack—
was holding his hand.

Her heart aching with love for him and for his children, Caidy walked down the aisle beside her brother to
the beautiful strains of the music toward a future filled
with joy and laughter and song.

* * * * *

REQUEST YOUR FREE BOOKS!

2 FREE NOVELS PLUS 2 FREE GIFTS!

 Harlequin®

SPECIAL EDITION

Life, Love & Family

YES! Please send me 2 FREE Harlequin® Special Edition novels and my 2 FREE gifts (gifts are worth about $10). After receiving them, if I don't wish to receive any more books, I can return the shipping statement marked "cancel." If I don't cancel, I will receive 6 brand-new novels every month and be billed just $4.49 per book in the U.S. or $5.24 per book in Canada. That's a saving of at least 14% off the cover price! It's quite a bargain! Shipping and handling is just 50¢ per book in the U.S. and 75¢ per book in Canada.* I understand that accepting the 2 free books and gifts places me under no obligation to buy anything. I can always return a shipment and cancel at any time. Even if I never buy another book, the two free books and gifts are mine to keep forever.

235/335 HDN FEGF

Name	(PLEASE PRINT)	
Address		Apt. #
City	State/Prov.	Zip/Postal Code

Signature (if under 18, a parent or guardian must sign)

Mail to the **Reader Service:**
IN U.S.A.: P.O. Box 1867, Buffalo, NY 14240-1867
IN CANADA: P.O. Box 609, Fort Erie, Ontario L2A 5X3

Not valid for current subscribers to Harlequin Special Edition books.

Want to try two free books from another line?
Call 1-800-873-8635 or visit www.ReaderService.com.

* Terms and prices subject to change without notice. Prices do not include applicable taxes. Sales tax applicable in N.Y. Canadian residents will be charged applicable taxes. Offer not valid in Quebec. This offer is limited to one order per household. All orders subject to credit approval. Credit or debit balances in a customer's account(s) may be offset by any other outstanding balance owed by or to the customer. Please allow 4 to 6 weeks for delivery. Offer available while quantities last.

Your Privacy—The Reader Service is committed to protecting your privacy. Our Privacy Policy is available online at www.ReaderService.com or upon request from the Reader Service.

We make a portion of our mailing list available to reputable third parties that offer products we believe may interest you. If you prefer that we not exchange your name with third parties, or if you wish to clarify or modify your communication preferences, please visit us at www.ReaderService.com/consumerschoice or write to us at Reader Service Preference Service, P.O. Box 9062, Buffalo, NY 14269. Include your complete name and address.

HSE11B

THE OTHER SIDE OF US
A brand-new novel
from Harlequin® Superromance® author
Sarah Mayberry

*In recovery from a serious accident, Mackenzie Williams
is beating all the doctors' predictions. But she needs
single-minded focus. She doesn't need the distraction
of neighbors—especially good-looking ones
like Oliver Garrett!*

MACKENZIE BREATHED DEEPLY to recover from the workout. She'd pushed herself too far but she wanted to accelerate her rehabilitation. Still, she needed to lie down to combat the nausea and shaking muscles.

There was a knock on the front door. Who on earth would be visiting her on a Thursday morning? Probably a cold-calling salesperson.

She answered, but her pithy rejection died before she'd formed the first words.

The man on her doorstep was definitely not a cold caller. Nothing about this man was cold, from the auburn of his wavy hair to his brown eyes to his sensual mouth. Nothing cold about those broad shoulders, flat belly and lean hips, either.

"Hey," he said in a shiver-inducing baritone. "I'm Oliver Garrett. I moved in next door." His smile was so warm and vibrant it was almost offensive.

"Mackenzie Williams." Oh, no. Her legs were starting to

tremble, indicating they wouldn't hold up long. Any second now she would embarrass herself in front of this complete and very good-looking stranger.

"It's been years since I was down here." He seemed to settle in for a chat. "It doesn't look as though—"

"I have to go." Her stomach rolled as she shut the door. The last thing she registered was the look of shock on Oliver's face at her abrupt dismissal.

And somehow she knew their neighborly relations would be a lot cooler now.

*Will Mackenzie be able to make it up to Oliver
for her rude introduction?
Find out in THE OTHER SIDE OF US
by Sarah Mayberry, available January 2013 from
Harlequin® Superromance®. PLUS, exciting changes are
in the works! Enjoy the same great stories in a longer
format and new look—beginning January 2013!*

HSREXP1212HH